AS MUCH AS I KNOW

Random House New York

As Much As
I KNOW

Susan Thames

Grateful acknowledgment is made to Arc Music for permission to re-
print excerpts from "Dearest Darling" by Ellas McDaniel. Copyright
© 1958 (renewed) by Arc Music Corporation. All rights reserved.
Reprinted by permission.

Library of Congress Cataloging-in-Publication Data
Thames, Susan.
As much as I know : stories / Susan Thames
p.   cm.
ISBN 0-679-40495-3
1. Women—Fiction.   I. Title.
PS3570.H3184A7   1992
813'.54—dc20   91-52688

Manufactured in the United States of America
9 8 7 6 5 4 3 2
First Edition

Book design by Lilly Langotsky

FOR CHRIS, LINSEY, JOY, AND LINDA

Contents

AS MUCH AS I KNOW

If There's Anything
You Want to Know

Winter, blue cold winter, winter so bare she can't remember summer and when she does she can't believe it will ever come again. Riding the train from Welch to Roanoke, Emma sees mile after mile of winter from her window seat atop the pile of coats her mother has set her on. The sight of the hairy frost and ice on the ground is like a screech in her brain and gives her the shivers, just like when Petey rides the teetertotter. It's rusted and squeaks so shrill it feels like her face is breaking. Her mother said her father has to oil it, but he never did and now he's in Roanoke with Papa and Nanny and they see him only on weekends. Petey rides it anyway and laughs at

Emma when she sticks her fingers in her ears. But not these days because it's too cold out.

These days they mostly just go for walks up behind their white house with green shutters, up in the woods where Emma once saw her mother walking with Artie Rose. Artie lives next door with his wife, Estelle, who is cross-eyed but has a very good figure. Her mother said no, it wasn't Artie Rose, because she was walking alone. Maybe Emma saw the ghost of the man who was buried by his people in the garden up the hill because they say that Artie Rose bears him a strong resemblance is what Emma's mother told her. Emma said oh, well, she'd only seen the ghost at night before and maybe he looked different in the daytime. Emma's mother said, "Hmmm," and kissed Emma's cheek with stiff, dry lips. Emma told her mother she'd take a better look next time, as a matter of fact she'd been trying to talk to him because she'd like to get to know him. "Why," her mother asked, "would you want to be friends with a ghost?"

Emma thought for a while, even though she already knew the answer. "Because he knows things other people don't know."

"If there's anything you want to know, you just ask me," her mother said, and she gave Emma's nose a little tweak.

Emma listens carefully to the whistle of the train. It's the sound of a song a dozen people are singing at the same time, but each person is singing a different note. The car is filled with rows and rows of nubby, reddish-brown seats, worn and scratchy. It smells like cigarettes and grown men, it burns the back of Emma's throat, and she thinks she might sneeze.

She wishes they were riding in their car to Roanoke, because you can stop whenever you want. Like at the filling station where their father once stopped and everybody except Emma's mother got out to look at the maps and the big cooler full of Coca-Cola and Nehi. Inside, there was a couple of chairs in front of a little coal stove where you could sit down and get warm, only it was July and the door was open and the place was full of flies and there wasn't a fire in the stove. Over by the cooler, a man with a bushy mustache was playing "The Mississippi Mud" on a banjo that had only two strings and Petey did a stomping dance on the dusty floor, pumping his elbows like a chicken and making everybody laugh. Emma wishes they were with their father in their car, but he sold the car and now they always take the train.

The ride from Welch to Roanoke is five hours with all the stops. At the station in Bluefield a lady is standing on the platform. For a while she looks at the engine and then she runs back through the station out to the road and waves her hand, waves both her hands at the black sedan moving slowly over the gravel away from the station. She grips her small valise under her arm and runs down the road, pressing her red hat to her head with her free hand. Emma's mother is chewing the eraser of a yellow pencil and reading a recipe in *Family Circle*, so when Emma tells her that the lady is the

5

daughter of the ghost her mother just says, "Uh huh," and doesn't tighten her lips.

Soon they will be at Emma's favorite part of the trip, where the train crosses a big valley on a trestle wide enough for just one train and all the pointy-topped pine trees in the world carpet the floor and the walls of the valley in green. Last Friday Emma saw a boy hanging off the side of the trestle, holding onto the wooden beam and peering down to the floor of the valley. Emma told Petey the boy was trying to see which house he wanted to live in next because he just went from house to house, living with different people all the time and telling stories for the families so they would let him stay. Petey said he already knew about the boy, but Emma knew he was lying. She said, "I love to hear you lie," and smiled at him like a crazy lady, which was the thing that Petey hated the most.

Emma is trying to wait until they get to the valley so she can count how many hidden chimneys are sending up lazy ribbons of smoke through the dense pinewood, but she has to pee bad. She knows how to squeeze her legs together real tight and it doesn't matter if some comes out, because her leggings are thick so it doesn't show. In the summertime she has to be more careful. Once she saw a man on a bus who peed in his pants and he didn't think it showed, but when he stood up he stuck his butt out and then she could see it plain as day. Sometimes she can tell Petey doesn't shake good after he pees and there's a little spot on his trousers, but it always dries fast.

"Emma, do you have to go to the bathroom?" her mother asks her.

"Yes, ma'am, but I want to wait until we get to the trestle because that's my best part of the trip."

"Well, sugar, that's still a ways off. Let's go to the bathroom. We'll get back in plenty of time."

In her heart Emma knows her mother is wrong. While they are walking to the front of the car a little comes out.

The bathroom is only a tiny toilet with a hard black seat. Her mother spreads two long strips of paper on the seat and holds them in place while Emma sits down. She has to wait a while before she can pee, which is funny because before it was coming out without even trying, but now it's gone. Her mother says, "Think of the pony," and they both laugh because once Artie took Emma and Petey and their mother for a pony ride and one of the ponies peed for so long Artie said he could put out a fire.

Remembering the pony works. After Emma wipes, she buckles the suspenders on her leggings and waits for her mother to pee. "Once James Harding didn't pee for two weeks and his peter swelled up like a big turnip and his mother had to cut it off," Emma says.

"Hush," her mother says. "Who told you such a thing?"

"The ghost," Emma answers.

"I've heard enough about that ghost," her mother says.

When they open the door to the bathroom they are already into the curve of the trestle. Emma counts smoke rising from seven secret chimneys while she hums "Yankee Doodle" to

7

herself, quiet as she can so that Petey won't hear because if he does, he will sing some other song very loud and she will lose the tune.

Their mother takes out lunch. They are having cream-cheese-and-jelly sandwiches. Each sandwich is neatly wrapped in a small square of gingham and tied up with string because it's foolish not to use what can be reused. Emma has her sandwich cut in four little squares, which she likes to eat in four bites each. Across the aisle, a small, dark-skinned man, the only other person in the car besides Emma, Petey, and their mother, is eating bananas. Emma counts one banana for every square of her sandwich. He's colored but he's not a Negro. Emma asks her mother why he's in the white people's car. Her mother says he's from India. Emma looks at the man again. Then she tells her mother he's in trouble because he was mistaken for the dwarf from the circus who set the elephants free and now the police are looking for him. Emma's mother says nonsense and makes her lips skinny. Emma turns her face toward the window and imitates her mother like her father does sometimes, drawing her lips wide across her face and squeezing her eyes up tight so that everything streaks into a glittering silvery flash.

After lunch Emma gets sleepy. Her mother covers her with the Persian lamb coat that used to belong to Nanny. The tight silver curls are like little cushiony stars against her cheek. Emma sleeps and the next thing she knows they are in Roanoke. She climbs down off the seat and reaches her arms into the gray quilted lining of her coat. Her mother buckles

8

the belt and turns up the collar so that the soft woolly fur brushes Emma's chin. Emma's mother says that hand-me-downs are nothing to be ashamed of, and it doesn't matter that the coat used to be Petey's, and anyway, she says she really bought it for Emma but she was still too little to wear it so Petey used it until Emma grew into it. Emma smooths down the flaps of the pockets with her hands stuffed into her mittens. Her mother takes one of Emma's hands and Petey carries their travel case. The conductor helps everyone down but the Indian man. He uses the railing and stands on the path looking for someone with only his hat in his hand.

Emma's grandmother waves her walking stick from alongside the car and her grandfather blows them a kiss from his seat on the front bumper. Their father is waiting on the platform, chewing his gum on one side of his mouth, smiling on the other, standing like he always does with his long knobby fingers on his hips and his long legs set wide apart. When he catches Emma up in his arms and swings her around in a circle, her feet reach out from her ankles like little wings. After he sets her down he puts his arms around her mother and roughs her up a bit. That's his way with her. She pouts and tucks her chin till he reaches under and lifts it up and kisses her, which is when Petey says, "Yuck," so their father has to pay attention to him. Up in the air Petey goes, too, over his father's shoulder till he is hanging upside down. He laughs so hard he is crying. Their mother says, "Paul, be careful, you'll hurt him," and he sets Petey down again and Petey says, "More, more."

On the ride home in the turquoise-and-white Buick, Emma's grandparents want to know everything about the trip. Emma talks about the Indian man, and about the little paper cups for cold water and how many chimneys she saw smoking in the valley. But she is also trying to listen to her father talking to her mother about Cyril, who is a relative of her father's, and about Connecticut, which is not Virginia and not West Virginia. "Cyril won't charge any rent on the store for the first year," her father says, "and he's found us a house, a side-by-side that's close to town, walking distance to school for Petey and Emma. Not much more to do now but pack and we're on our way."

"You make it sound like he's offering you the sun, the moon, and the stars," her mother says in a voice she uses only for special times when she wants to get things to go her way and being sweet won't work.

Emma squeezes her father's hand real hard. He looks down at her, smiles, strokes her hair, and whispers, "Don't you worry about none of this, angel. Everything is going to be just fine."

"That's right, everything *is* going to be just fine because we aren't going anywhere, leastways, we aren't going all the way clear up to Connecticut, so far away from all our people and . . ."

"But Cyril is *family,* Lorraine," her father says. He's being gentle now and touching Emma's mother like he is touching Emma. "When we were kids, Cyril came and lived with us

when his father was out of work, came more than once, two
or three times. Now he feels . . ."

"I know all about yours and Cyril's and Sam's hard times.
But it's not the same thing, giving a spare bed to a kid and
promising a living to a man with a family."

Petey is asking all kinds of questions—can he get a scooter,
do they have a lake, and about snow—all kinds of questions,
like he knows what's going on. Then he reaches back between
the seats and pinches Emma's leg, but she doesn't make a
sound.

In the kitchen of Nanny and Papa's apartment, Petey has
hot chocolate and listens to the radio. Emma takes off her
coat, tugs her way out of her leggings, and sits down at the
table to drink from the mug her grandmother sets down for
her. Petey is talking about Connecticut again, which is just
like him to talk about some place he's never been. Emma says,
"I don't care, because Nanny is going to take me into her
room and show me the special things and you can't come."

Emma's grandparents' bedroom is the brightest room in the
apartment. The corner has pale see-through lace curtains and
two big windows that crank open and shut with little metal
handles. Emma sits at the foot of one of the twin beds and
runs her hand over the silvery-blue bedspread. "How many
years have you and Papa slept in these beds?" Emma asks.

"Twenty-eight years come August," her grandmother says
as she opens the top drawer of her side of the bureau and
takes out a box covered in quilted blue satin. She sits down

next to Emma on the bed and raises the wide lid of the box. "This is the gift your grandfather brought me the first time he came to call on me," she begins. "We lived way out in the country. He drove to our house in an open roadster, and when he got there, he was covered with red dust from the summer-dried Georgia clay. I had to run into the bathroom and hide so he wouldn't see me laughing at him. Your great-grandmother let him wash in the kitchen, and when I came out, he gave me this lapel pin, which he got at the world's fair in San Diego."

"And then you married him and followed him to Roanoke and then your mother, my Great Nana Brenner, came to live with you," Emma says.

"Well, not quite that fast," her grandmother says, and she tickles Emma under her arms and pulls her a little closer.

Emma jumps down from the bed and faces her grandmother with her hands on her hips. "Is that a true story, Nanny?" she asks.

"Why, of course it's a true story," her grandmother answers. "Haven't I been telling you that story ever since you were little?" She pats the spot on the bed next to her and takes the next special thing from the open box. Emma nods her head with satisfaction, as though she has made a clear point of something, and takes her place again, pressing against her grandmother's softness. "Here," her grandmother begins once more, "is one of the gloves I wore when your grandfather and I were married."

Emma interrupts, "And the other one you threw to the handsome young broncobuster when the rodeo came to

Roanoke and you wish you had both the gloves now but he was the handsomest boy you ever saw and Papa didn't even get jealous or laugh at you when you cried later on over the lost glove."

"That's right. In a little while, this glove will be just the right size for you. Won't be much use, being only one; still, it will be yours."

Emma takes the yellowed white glove from her grandmother and runs her fingertips over the small pearls sewed to the cuff. Then she slips her hand in and out of the glove slowly. "Can I take the box with me to Connecticut, Nanny, or can you bring it to me there? Can you come with me?"

Her grandmother tightens her hold and presses Emma's face against her breast. It is a warm place, safer than any place Emma knows. Emma looks up at her grandmother and says, "Nanny, you know what? You want to hear something?" and her grandmother says, "Of course I do. I want to hear everything you want to tell me." Emma thinks she will tell her grandmother about the ghost, but she changes her mind and says, "I forgot."

The next day is Saturday and Emma's father has to go to work in the curtain shop with her grandfather. The day after that is Sunday and that's the best day because everybody is together in the morning and also for a big dinner of gooey chicken with potatoes and carrots and applesauce on the side. Emma's grandfather wears a starched short-sleeved white shirt and says a blessing before they eat and Emma thinks she can taste the blessing in the chicken.

But then it's the worst day because Emma and Petey and their mother put all their things back in the little tan case and go to the station to get the train back to Welch. Their father walks them right up to their compartment and helps each of them onto the train. Back out on the platform, he finds them at their window seats and motions for their mother to raise the window, but it's stuck. Still, Emma can hear him when he says, "I love you, Lorraine." And of course she hears her mother when she says, "Okay, Paul."

It's already dark by the time the train leaves the station. The tiny lights that dot the countryside seem as far away as the stars. Emma looks out the window but all she sees is her own face showing back at her, except when she presses her nose up against the glass, but then the darkness makes swirling pools behind her eyes and something like rolling water in her throat, so she makes up a game with the words to "Oh, Say Can You See" and the tune to "Bless This House."

When it isn't winter but not yet spring, Emma and her mother and Petey stop going to Roanoke on weekends and their father comes back to Welch for the two days instead. They all work Saturday and Sunday, packing up boxes of china and glasses and books and making piles of things they fold—towels, curtains, bedspreads, all their clothes—and putting them in boxes too. After a while the house gets to looking like nobody lives there anymore. Emma stands in her empty room and tries to remember all the things that filled it only yesterday, or the day before.

During the week, Emma's mother talks on the phone, or speaks rudely to somebody else on the party line, saying she has a personal emergency, yes, *another* personal emergency. Once she snaps, "Well, we *are* moving, you know, and all kinds of things come up when you're getting ready to move." Then she makes her call, or she waits by the phone for someone to call her, and after she talks for a while, it's never very long, about long enough for ones and twos in a game of jacks, she cries quietly to herself, and then she makes a cup of tea.

Every afternoon their mother goes to get the mail from the mailbox and meet Emma and Petey at the school bus stop. One day she's waiting for them, but she's in a hurry and she shows them a large package wrapped in brown paper. Petey reads the return address but the only word that Emma recognizes is *Connecticut*. They walk and run up the road to their house, but Emma stays close to her mother and draws her hand back and forth across the brown paper.

Petey throws his coat off as he runs to the kitchen for the scissors. Their mother opens the wrapping paper carefully, then there is more string around the box, and the box has a lid and lots of tissue paper inside. Hidden in the tissue paper is a small black photograph album with gold around the edges and a card taped to the front. Petey reads, "Welcome to Watertown."

At the kitchen table, the three of them huddle over two dozen color pictures, each one stuck on the page with four little gold corner holders, pictures of Cousin Cyril and his family with everybody's names, including the dogs', who are Panama and Fedora. Emma's mother says those are kinds of hats and Watertown is where they make a lot of hats and that's how the dogs got their names. There are pictures of Cyril's big brick house, and his store, which has a Chinese restaurant with a pink neon sign right next to it, and a picture of the brown frame house where Emma and Petey and their mother and father will live. Emma's mother says what a nice picture it is, and how it looks like a very nice house, even if it is a little small and there isn't much of a yard.

Emma looks at the picture again, at the house, which looks very big to her, at the yard, which has no woods. She tries to know something about this place they are going to, or even to think of a question to ask, but there's nothing. Petey is full of questions—is there an attic, which bedroom is his, where is the snow. "This house is haunted," Emma says, looking at her mother with her eyes wide open and her brows raised high above her bangs.

"What a silly idea," her mother says. "Honestly, Emma, sometimes I just don't know what goes on in that head of yours."

The day before they leave, friends from the neighborhood come to the house to help load boxes and furniture and rolled-up rugs into the big van hitched on to the back of the new old car Emma's father has brought home from Roanoke. Emma's mother says she doesn't see how it will make it to Connecticut, but what do you expect for sixty dollars? Emma tells her mother that she doesn't want to go to Connecticut, that she'd just as soon stay in Roanoke with Nanny and Papa. Her mother says, "You will go exactly where you are taken, and don't you forget it, young lady." Emma pretends to herself that she has just changed her mind, that she will go to Connecticut and then she will go to Roanoke later on, in a week, or next year.

That night, Petey and Emma sleep on mattresses side by side in Emma's nearly empty room. They each have an extra quilt because it's cold on the floor and the windows are bare and outside a silent snow is falling on the shoots of the crocus bulbs and covering the ground and the big rocks with a dusting of white. Emma puts her clothes for the next day under the covers so they will be warm when she dresses in the morning. "That's the exactly right thing for a dummy to do," Petey says to her through slitted eyes. Then he lifts his quilts and sheet to show Emma that he is fully dressed for the morning, corduroy trousers, thick wool socks, and navy-blue sweater. Emma turns on her other side and ducks most of her head under the blanket and falls asleep.

In the morning Artie and Estelle take everybody to the diner in town for a big breakfast before they begin their long drive. Artie says they can have whatever they want. Emma and Petey have waffles and sausage with plenty of butter and syrup. Their father has a western omelet and two orders of toast and their mother has an English muffin and coffee.

When they go back to the house, Emma's mother goes inside to check all the cupboards and closets one more time. Their father hollers from the car, "Lorraine, if we leave

17

anything, the new folks will send it along. You've checked a hundred times."

Petey hollers, "Let's leave Emma," but Emma doesn't pay him any mind. She is on her way up to the woods behind the house, up to where the ghost might be; she just might get lucky, it's her last chance.

The woods seem larger than ever before, and lonelier too. Emma hugs a young birch tree and listens to her mother calling her. She feels a chill come over her, up from the ground beneath her boots. Her legs shake like twigs in a storm and her chin stutters in silence. Petey comes up beside her. He is breathing hard and there are big puff clouds of breath coming out of his mouth. He takes Emma's arms from around the tree, takes her hand in his, and guides her through the rocks and the broken branches of the woods to the backyard, around the side of the house, down the steps, and into the car.

Emma and Petey look for license plates from out-of-state cars. After they see their third car from Oklahoma, they start to tire of this game. Then they look for animals, which is even more boring because there isn't a groundhog or a rabbit spotted for the longest time. Just north of Cumberland Emma sees a chipmunk, but she can't remember the name. "There's one," she hollers, pulling hard on the back of her mother's seat and pointing out the window frantically.

"There's one what?" Petey asks.

"I don't know the name," she says. "It's little and has a brown stripe down its back. Look, you can still see it."

"I don't see anything," Petey says. "And if you mean a chipmunk, they don't have chipmunks in Maryland."

"Chipmunk, that's it. I saw a chipmunk," Emma says triumphantly.

"No, you didn't," Petey insists in his huffiest voice. "Artie said once we get above the Mason-Dixon line we won't see a lot of the animals we have back home. And chipmunks is one of them."

Their father pops a fresh piece of gum in his mouth and chuckles. "I don't imagine Artie said anything of the kind, Petey. Artie's a city boy. He wouldn't know a chipmunk if it bit his nose."

"Well, how do you like that," their mother says. "As a matter of fact, Artie Rose happens to know quite a lot about animals, both wild and domestic. They do have Four-H Clubs in Charleston, you know, and he learned more about animals than anybody I know."

Emma sits back in her seat with her chin propped on the door and her nose pressed against the window. All she has to do to settle this business is find another chipmunk. The sound of her mother's and father's voices blur like the trees that rush by along the road.

There's a stretch of the highway out and a detour that passes through a couple of towns filled with town things—houses, stores, schools, fire stations, dogs, a flagpole—just

19

like Welch. They stop at a rest stop near Carlisle. Their father gets out to check the water in the radiator and Emma rolls down her window. A woman is sitting on the picnic table set back under the trees and beside her is a little girl in a raggedy coat. On the ground near the woman are great bundles of clothes and blankets tied up with rope and a black guitar case on top of one of the bundles. The woman pokes some loose strands of brown hair into the braid at the back of her neck. Emma's father lowers the hood and gets back into the car. "Put your window up, Emma," he says as he turns the key in the ignition.

As she rolls up the window, Emma points to the woman standing by the side of the road and says to her brother, "That woman is the ghost of Joan of Arc."

Petey looks up from the map on his lap and says, "Ghosts don't have kids, smarty-pants."

"Since when do you know everything about ghosts?" Emma asks.

"I don't know everything about ghosts," he answers. "It's just common sense. If your mother died, would you turn into a ghost?"

"Would I?" Emma asks her mother.

"No, sugar," her mother says, "you most certainly would not."

"Kind of clever, just the same," her father says as he guides the car around a pothole marked with a bright yellow cone. "Where'd you hear about Joan of Arc?"

"I heard about her from Ar—" Emma leans on the back of

her mother's seat and breathes heavily against her neck. Her mother looks up from her nails and her pink emery board.

"What are you crowding me for?" her mother asks.

"For nothing." Emma sits back in her seat. "I don't remember where I heard about Joan of Arc. Maybe it was in school. There was a joke. Because of the boy named Jonah Park. That was it." Emma runs her finger back and forth on the chrome door latch. Billboards with pictures of swimming pools and lobster dinners fly by and the afternoon stretches on like a dream.

Just after dark they check into a little motel attached to a brightly lit diner where they can eat supper. Their room is small and after Emma and Petey wash their faces and hands and comb their hair, their mother sends them over to sit in the vestibule of the diner so their father can clean up and have a minute's rest.

A skinny man with a crew cut and a short tie shows them to a booth by the window. The waitress comes to take their order. She has red hair in tight curls that remind Emma of bicycle springs. Her name is written on the pocket of her uniform, "Judy." Emma's father orders first. "Well, Judy," he says, and he winks at Emma, "I'll have your Maryland crab cakes, if you please, with green beans and a baked potato."

Emma whispers across the table to Petey, "What are crab cakes?" and Petey kicks her. Emma kicks him back and takes the hand of her mother, who is ordering roast chicken with mashed potatoes, gravy, and lima beans. Petey asks can he have lamb. It's his favorite thing ever since he had supper at his friend Chip's house, but Emma's mother refuses to cook it because the smell is so disgusting. Their mother says yes, he can have it, but he better not come near her after dinner and Emma says, "And don't come near me either." Emma orders baked Virginia ham and Petey makes a horrible face like he is going to be sick.

While they are waiting for their food, their father puts a dime in the little jukebox just beneath the window at their table. When Patsy Cline starts singing "I'm Back in Baby's Arms," he takes their mother's hands across the table and does a pretend dance, swinging her hands back and forth, only she looks embarrassed and hardly moves at all. Petey is reading out loud about the state of Pennsylvania from the paper place mat in front of him. Emma is singing along with Patsy and trying to connect the dots on the place-mat game without a pencil.

Supper comes and everything is delicious. "The best thing about eating out is that everybody can have exactly what they want," Emma's father says.

"As long as it doesn't cost too much," Petey says.

"It's the best ham I ever ate," Emma says.

"Don't talk with your mouth full," her mother says and she presses Emma's lips closed with her fingers. Emma looks to see if Petey is laughing but his eyes are lowered to his dish.

There are two beds, one for their mother and father and one for Emma and Petey, and a radio on the nightstand with a lamp that has two heads. Emma and Petey's nightclothes are laid out on their bed and they are changed and under their covers fast, without a word.

Their mother is in the bathroom washing her hose in the basin. She is wearing her slip and one of her husband's old T-shirts to sleep. She comes to her side of the bed and lifts the covers. " 'Night, children," she says.

Their father is sitting on the edge of the bed in his undershorts and T-shirt, looking at the map. He puts out the lamp and turns on the radio. It makes a soft buzz that gently stings Emma's head. She watches the gold glow from the dial light his hand as he turns the knob. He stops. A horn is crying a song that sounds like someone is calling from far away to somebody who won't ever hear. Petey's breath is sweet with lamb and his hand is damp in hers. When the song is over, her father's long arm reaches out to turn off the radio. " 'Night, Emma."

Emma lies quietly, counting the drops of water as they fall from her mother's hose to the tile floor of the bathroom.

Her mother keeps Emma home from Watertown Elementary School. Next fall is soon enough for her to start, she says, and Emma can help setting up the house. At least once a day they ride the bus down Main Street past the market and get off at Hillside Avenue and walk to Cyril's house. Along the way, her mother points out her favorite houses to Emma and says where everybody's bedrooms would be and what color she'd pick for the living-room wallpaper. When they get to number 39 they sit with Cyril's wife, Maryrose, who really is rosy and gentle and has what Emma's mother says is alto-gether too much patience with her two little hot-dog dogs. Emma's mother says how they're getting on and Maryrose always asks if there's anything they need and Emma's mother says "How kind of you to ask," or "Not a thing in the world," but they always leave with something, a bed sheet, a spatula, a can of tomatoes, a throw rug.

Today they stop at the store to bring her father his lunch. He leads them down the aisles of tables piled high with bolts of fabric, plaids and checks and flowered prints, to a little corner in the back where he puts up water for tea on the hot plate. Then he clears a place for Emma and her mother to sit down, but her mother stands by the desk and looks at the green and yellow papers covered with columns of numbers. "Don't worry about any of that, Lorraine. I'm going to stay late tonight and work on the books," he says.

The little bell on the front door rings and Emma's mother says, "Sounds like you have a customer, Paul. I'll pour the water for the tea. Why don't you see to your customer."

"They'll holler if they need something. I'm going to stay right here and visit with the two prettiest girls in Watertown, two smartest girls, too," her father says, and he reaches an arm to each of them. Emma lets him pull her close, but her mother shuffles through some more papers on the desk and makes soft clucking noises between her teeth, which Emma imitates silently just to see what it feels like.

On the way home Emma's mother stops to look at the notions in the window of the J.J. Newberry's, which faces the square of the farmers' market. Emma stares at two girls standing by a stall where a small old woman with whiskers is selling little medals hung on purple thread and brilliantly colored pictures wrapped in cellophane. The girls, beautiful and dark like Gypsies, are whispering to each other. The smaller one is pulling at the other girl's sleeve, trying to get her away from the table. Then the taller one reaches her hand out fast and sweeps the medals and pictures from the table. As they clatter to the ground, she runs across the square, shouting, "Hurry! Hurry up!" The woman tending the table cries out after them, but no one pays her any mind. She kneels to pick up her goods, muttering under her troubled breath and shaking her fist in the air. Emma watches until the two girls are out of sight and then takes a step or two toward the table.

"Where are you going, young lady?" her mother asks.

"I want to look at the pictures on that table," Emma says.

"Those are just prayer cards," her mother says. "Let's go inside. I have to buy some straight pins."

"What are prayer cards?" Emma asks.

"Foolishness is what they are," her mother says, steering Emma toward the door. "Prayers for people who believe in saints and angels and all kinds of nonsense."

"And ghosts?" Emma asks.

"Probably ghosts too," her mother says.

"We believe in ghosts," Emma says.

Her mother rolls her eyes and shakes her head. "Never mind, Emma."

At home there is mail in the mailbox outside their door. Emma pores carefully over a catalog filled with pictures of ladies' clothes and underwear and tries to imagine having the parts to put inside the funny girdles and brassieres. Her mother sits on the chair by the front door and reads a letter typewritten on white paper. When she is through, she folds it carefully and kisses it. Then she puts it in the pocket of her apron. "Who's the letter from?" Emma asks.

"Your grandmother," her mother answers. "Everybody is fine. She sends you her love. And she says she's coming to visit this summer."

Emma puts her arms around her mother's neck and says, "Isn't that good? Aren't you happy?"

Her mother gives her a big hug and says, "Yes, sweetheart, I'm very happy."

In the afternoon, Emma cuts pictures from a stack of old magazines she found in the cellar while her mother does the ironing. They listen to the radio and sing the songs they know. Sometimes Emma's mother sets her iron on its end and leads Emma to the middle of the kitchen floor and twirls her and spins her till she is out of breath. They are dancing when Emma's father opens the front door and calls hello to them.

Her mother drops Emma's hands. "How can you be home so early?" she asks Emma's father.

"How could I stay away is more the question," he says. He sets a box filled with yellow and green pieces of paper down on the kitchen table and takes Emma's mother in his arms, all set to dance to the tune on the radio.

Emma's mother pulls her lips back tight over her teeth and raises her eyebrows nearly to a point. "Not now, Paul," she says. "Emma, put your coat on and go outside and play till suppertime."

From the back porch, Emma can see beyond a dozen back-yards, past alleyways, turned-over garbage cans, and dead trees, all the way down to Main Street. At the corner there is a traffic light that blinks yellow both ways. Emma is trying to count how many times it blinks in a minute but the clock on the tower of the First Congregationalist Church moves in big jumps. It is already twenty-five past four and Petey is late. He has trombone lessons with Mr. Griffey on Fridays, but he is usually home by four o'clock.

When the telephone rings, Emma's mother answers the call. Emma presses her chin against the top of a brown shingle and watches and listens through the window open only an inch at the bottom. Her mother is sitting on one of the kitchen chairs with her feet twisted around the front legs of the chair, biting her bottom lip, the telephone gripped tightly in her hand. After a while she shakes her head and says a few words and hangs up. Emma's father spits his gum out and stands at the sink running a glass of water. Her mother gets up and puts on her apron. "You can't even provide a little pleasure for your son. I told you this would happen, damn you," she says, and though her voice is quiet, her words are clear like they were spoken, each one of them, so close to Emma that her mother's breath tickles her ear.

Emma turns from the window to look down the hill to Main

Street. She taps her foot against the railing in time to the Sousa march that Petey is learning while she plays the tune very loudly in her head. "And tell her to come in and help with supper," Emma's mother is saying when Petey opens the back door.

Petey closes the door behind him. He sits down on the top step of the porch and shoots make-believe pebbles into the yard. "No more trombone lessons," he says.

"How come?" Emma asks.

"Not till after we get squared away, that's what Mama says, not till after she finds a job and we catch up."

"I thought the lessons came free," Emma says.

"They do but you have to pay two dollars a month for the trombone," Petey explains.

Emma looks at the fat pads of Petey's fingers and remembers how he grips the slide of the shiny brass trombone, his cheeks round and red, remembers how the trombone stutters behind his lips until one long deep note pours out of its bell and into the room. She sits down next to him and holds him while he cries.

"Where did you hear such a story?" their mother asks Petey at breakfast on Saturday.

"A boy at school told about it. He says he read it in a newspaper, and he told another story too, about a man who killed his wife, shot her with a slingshot, hit her right between the . . ."

"That's enough," their mother says. "I don't want to hear

another word about it. For pity's sake, it's gotten to where you can't believe a thing you read. Slingshot, indeed."

"You believe what you read," Emma says to her mother. "Leastways, you believe what comes in the mail."

"What came in the mail?" Petey asks.

"A letter from Nanny," Emma answers.

"What did she say?" Petey asks as he picks the raisins from his cereal.

"Said she was coming this summer, didn't she, Mama?" Emma says.

"Not exactly," her mother answers.

"What about the letter?" Emma says. "Didn't you say the letter said she was coming?"

"I made a mistake," their mother says, getting up from the table to pour herself more hot water for another cup of tea. "No, she didn't say that. She might be coming. But that isn't what the letter was about."

"But you said . . ." Emma goes on.

"I know what I said, but now I'm saying something else. Now I'm saying that I don't want to talk about this and I don't want you talking about it either. Emma, eat your toast." She pushes Emma's plate a little closer to her till it is nearly falling off the table. Emma gives it a little nudge with her chest to save it from her lap.

After they finish their chores, Emma and Petey play with Petey's rubber soldiers on his bed, in the folds of the sheets and the quilt, with the pillow and two flannel shirts for a fortress and mountain ranges.

"What else did the boy at school say?" Emma asks. They are arranging their men in foxholes and behind fallen buildings.

"About what?"

"About the man who shot his wife, what else did he tell you?"

"Nothing much. Except that the lady was a deaf-mute and never talked except once she started to scream and she couldn't stop so he shot her and she still didn't stop screaming and he got scared that maybe she was dead and the scream wouldn't ever end so he shot her nine more times, to make the screaming stop. That's all."

"That's nothing," Emma says. "They have worse things than that in the Bible. I have to pee. No attacking me before I get back."

The bathroom mirror is the door of the medicine cabinet and over it is the light. The light goes on and off with the switch by the door, or else with the beaded chain that hangs down from the bulb shaded by a pink paper ruffle that looks like the bottom of Emma's mother's best summer dress. Emma pushes the wall switch up but the light doesn't go on. She tries it again, on and off, and then she climbs up on the rim of the bathtub and stretches to pull the chain. The pink light shows Emma her own wide-mouthed face only two inches from the mirror and she gives a start of surprise. After her heart stops pounding she closes her eyes and puts her hands over her ears and presses down hard till there is a dull ringing in her head. In the darkness, she sees the backyard in Welch, the tall brown grasses, the ghost running into the woods, looking at

30

Emma over his shoulder, waving a letter at her and laughing.

"Emma, what are you doing up there?" Emma's mother asks. She is standing by the bathroom door putting neatly folded pink towels and washcloths on a shelf in the closet. Her apron strings are hanging at her sides and her sweater is buttoned crooked. "I saved the potatoes for you, Emma. 'Bout time to start dinner. Wash your hands and come on down-stairs."

Emma watches her reflection answer, "Yes, ma'am. Soon as I pee. And can I play one more game with Petey?"

"Yes, you can. Or you can come down and peel the potatoes and then go back to your game with Petey. Either way."

"I have to do the potatoes," Emma tells Petey. "But I can play one more game."

While they are rearranging their armies Petey asks, "What about Nanny?"

"You mean about the letter?" Emma says. "It was in the mail yesterday."

"How do you know it was from Nanny?" he says.

"Mama said so," Emma says.

"What did it look like?" Petey says. "Was it on blue paper with blue ink?"

"No," Emma says, "it was from a typewriter, and it was on white paper."

"You're putting your soldiers in my territory," Petey says.

"They're scouts," Emma says.

"No scouts allowed," Petey hollers in Emma's face. "You're a cheater. I don't want to play anymore."

31

"We always had scouts before," Emma cries to Petey.

"Only in the first battle," Petey screams at her. "You're a liar and a cheater," he says and he grabs the corner of the blanket and throws it off the bed and dozens of soldiers scatter across the floor. "Get out of my room."

Emma dries her eyes on her way down the stairs. Her mother is listening to the radio and reading the paper. After Emma finishes with the potatoes, she pulls a chair alongside her mother's and asks her mother to please find the comic strips for her. Sometimes when she goes to meet Petey on his way home from school, she stops at the newsstand on the corner of Main and White where Mrs. Topilsky lets her read the tattered funny papers left over from Sunday. Afternoons, her boy Benny comes in to give her a hand. Once he put his arm around his mother and said, "How you doing, Ma?"

Mrs. Topilsky laughed out loud. Then she turned to Emma and said, "Ain't he a good boy?"

Emma looks at her mother and says, "We don't say 'ain't,' do we?"

"No, darling," her mother answers.

"Why don't we say 'ain't'?" Emma asks.

"Because it's not good English," her mother says.

"What do we say instead?" Emma asks.

"We say, 'aren't,' " her mother says, turning the page of the paper.

"Aren't," Emma says. "Aren't I a good girl?" she says.

"Yes, darling," her mother says, "you're a very good girl."

Lorna Mitchell's Vision

There never was such a slow-moving train. More like it isn't moving at all. Even the morning mist is hanging over the engine like it's waiting for the train to move before it falls. Nearby, great low clouds cling to the walls of the valley, still as a drape at a closed window. Lorna Mitchell hugs her valise to her chest and curls her toes inside her new red pumps. The train may never come. She may never feel the conductor's hand on her elbow, helping her up the four steps onto the train, or feel the rough wool seat covers of the Norfolk and Western 11:40 to Roanoke. She may stand here on this platform forever, aching to go, longing to stay, never having to choose.

Never having to choose—and wouldn't that be the best? No more weighing the past against the future or guessing at what *might* be. And what might there be for a twenty-three-year-old hairdresser in a city of 100,000 people? Everything. At least that's what Darla Crawford says. All those people, and Lorna bursting with new ideas too big for Bluefield. All those shops, and theaters, road shows, the Ice Capades. There's even a Catholic church. A young woman could make her way in a place like Roanoke, if she wanted to, if she had vision.

Lorna had vision, that was certain. Hadn't she won every prize in the high school art department? And there wasn't anything more creative than her hair styling. The walls of the kitchen were covered with pictures of Lorna alongside her customers. Her mother told her it was conceited, but Lorna didn't pay her mother any mind, because when somebody came to the house for a cut and a set, looking at something a little different, there was inspiration in the pictures of the brides and bridesmaids in the three weddings Lorna did over the summer, and the dozen graduating high school seniors, with their near-perfect perms and flips of absolutely every length and color. There was no doubt about it, Lorna had a way of looking at things that was special, too special for Bluefield.

Even her mother said she was wasting herself in Bluefield on people who didn't appreciate her—and didn't her mother know what that was like?—people like Wayne Lucas, and what was he anyway? Nothing but a driver for some big shot from the electric company. That Cadillac he drove around wasn't his any more than the fine apartment over Mr.

Johnson's garage. Where was a job like that going to lead him? In ten years he might get a new jacket with shiny buttons to wear behind the wheel of some new Cadillac, but he'd never have anything of his own making. It wasn't enough that he had the deepest blue eyes in the valley.

But how could Lorna discount those eyes, or the way she felt on the floor of the VFW, dancing in his arms?

"Would you like to dance, Lorna?" he had asked, and although it was late and most everyone was rubbing their eyes and reaching for their sweaters and scarfs, Lorna said yes, but not without teasing him.

"Why do you come around pestering me again?" she asked.

He winked at her and answered, "Nobody else here fool enough to dance with me."

Lorna didn't feel a fool. For one thing, nobody could talk the way Wayne Lucas could, or make the weather sound interesting or a sigh sound like news. But that was what everybody knew about Wayne. Lorna knew other things: that there'd never been another man who felt the same as Wayne, who moved inside his trousers as if he wasn't dressed at all, like even when he was standing right next to you he was still coming at you. She'd listen to him talk about anything just to be near him.

As they made circles around the room, Wayne asked her, "Did you hear about the party the Johnsons had for their daughter Kitty Alice?"

"Not the particulars," Lorna answered. "Was it very lovely?"

35

"Loveliest party I've ever seen," he began, as Lorna settled into his arms and his voice, sinking deeper with each word. "Sweet sixteen, it was. Everything was pink. There was great armfuls of pink roses everywhere, even in the bathrooms, and pink candy, little ribbons of bright pink hard candy and pale pink candy wafers. The punch was pink, even the ice cubes floating in the big silver punch bowl were pink." Wayne's fingers gripped her tighter around her waist as he made a sudden turn and dip, and her heart brushed the floor. "There was a pink birthday cake, of course," he went on, "looked like a wedding cake, four tiers high, with dozens of candles on every tier, and sixteen special candles sparkling with pink glitter on the very top. And of course, Miss Kitty's dress was pink. Would you like to hear about her dress?"

His question seemed to wake her from a dream, though awake she couldn't remember the dream, only the feeling it left, of her body heavy, falling helplessly and then unresistingly into a tide of endless waves. Lorna took a deep breath to find her voice. "I would so like to hear about her dress."

"It was velvet."

"Honestly?"

"I swear. Baby-girl-pink velvet. Fitted tight as a glove on top, and the neckline scooped way low, the skirt went all the way down to the floor, yards of pink velvet moving around her feet." Then he pulled her a little closer so his chin was grazing the top of her head—she could feel his words rippling through her hair. "And the whole thing was trimmed in baby-girl-pink fur, dyed to match the dress, fur like feathers on her

36

shoulders and at her wrists and sweeping the floor with the hem of her dress with every step she took."

Lorna's heart was pounding so hard she thought she might faint. Wayne's hand was hot and damp through her dress. Her breasts felt full and hard against his chest and her back arched with longing as they finished the dance without another word.

He walked her to where her mother was standing. She was holding Lorna's sweater over her arm and saying goodnight to Mrs. DeRosa. Mrs. Mitchell smiled at Wayne and handed Lorna her sweater. Then Leonard Newton called the last dance. Mrs. Mitchell interrupted herself in the middle of a sentence to Mrs. DeRosa and turned to Wayne. "Well, Mr. Lucas, I make it my business never to sit out the last dance. Now I'm making it your business, too."

"Well, isn't she something?" Mrs. DeRosa asked Lorna. "Still knows how to have a good time for herself, doesn't she?" Lorna felt a catch somewhere, in her throat, her chest, her belly, as she watched her mother and Wayne dancing, talking like old friends. She was part proud, part shamed, and part something else, seeing her mother flirt with a man ten years younger than her. Of course, there was no harm in it. Lorna didn't have any claim on Wayne. Besides, it was just her mother. She did love to dance, and her father never would come to a single party or social. So what if her mother had been about the prettiest girl in Bluefield twenty years ago? Where had it got her? she was always asking Lorna. Whereas Lorna had enough good looks to get by and a whole lot more.

37

Lorna buffed the toes of her shoes against the backs of her socks and stood smiling, waiting for the dance to finish.

It never did amount to much, Lorna and Wayne. There was that dance, and then a couple of Sunday afternoon rides when he came to pick her up in the Cadillac, sharing with her his one afternoon off in the whole week. They drove around till it got dark, with the heater up and the radio on, laughing about how wide the front seat of the car was and how if she didn't move a little closer he was going to need a megaphone. One Sunday, he even stopped the car and they danced alongside the road to "Sea of Love," Wayne's hand wandering across her back like he was learning her, studying her, and she was yielding up all her secrets. Afterward, of course, they made awful fun of each other. But there'd also been the time she bumped into him in town when she was shopping with her mother. That was different from the other times, confusing. In all the world, she knew she wasn't that important to Wayne, but standing on that corner, she thought he'd be as warm toward her as he always was when they rode in the Cadillac. Instead, he was just the other side of friendly. You couldn't call it rude, he was much too well mannered for that, but it was enough to make her hope her mother didn't notice, or wouldn't say anything if she did.

It was right after the meeting in town that Lorna got an especially exciting letter from Darla on beautiful white stationery with "Hotel Patrick Henry" printed at the top in royal-blue ink. Darla wrote all about her job at the front desk of the hotel, about the new Hieronymous Department Store and the boy from Lynchburg who worked in the shoe department. She told about the fine restaurants, how the sparkle of the crystal and the silver on the tables was enough to make you dizzy just looking through the windows. She begged Lorna to come for a visit, to see the beauty salons, and talk to a few people about work, maybe at the shop right in the hotel. They could walk to work together. Wouldn't that be perfect?

Lorna figured that if she saved every penny, didn't buy new hose every time she got a run, worked for Theresa Sherman in her shop two nights a week—Theresa had been trying to get Lorna to come in with her ever since Lorna graduated from cosmetology school—she'd have the money for a trip by early spring, just in time to see all the dogwood in bloom. She was already imagining herself fussing over platinum-blond heads in a shop with big baskets of silk flowers and quality music on a hi-fi, a dozen customers competing for her Friday afternoon appointments.

At first her mother didn't have much to say about it, except that she thought Darla tended to be a little wild. Then, suddenly, she started to make phone calls and write letters, renewing old acquaintances, asking practically everybody she knew, "Don't you have a brother in Roanoke?" or "Is your wife's family still in Roanoke?" She told Lorna it didn't make sense to go just for a visit. How much could she tell about life in Roanoke if she didn't stay a while? Didn't Theresa know somebody with an opening in a shop out on Williamson Road, and didn't Louella Lester have an aunt right on the bus line with a room to rent? Before long, it seemed like moving to Roanoke had been what Lorna was aiming for all along.

Her father brought up the subject of Wayne. Lorna didn't think her father noticed much. He was usually tired from the long days he put in at the paper mill and he spent most of his nights with his good ear inches away from the radio, listening to whatever news he'd raise hell about over breakfast the next day.

It was at breakfast one morning when Lorna's mother was going on about Lorna's plans and Lorna's talent and Lorna's future. "What about Lorna's fellow?" he asked.

"What fellow?" her mother asked, before Lorna could say a word.

"That Wayne Lucas she's been seeing, that's what fellow. Don't tell me you didn't notice, Belle."

"Oh, Mama's noticed, Daddy. It's just that he's not really, I mean, we're not really . . . The thing of it is, I just saw him a few times." Lorna took a bite of her toast.

"I know that," her father went on, "but it seemed to me you two enjoyed one another more than a little. You told me he thought the idea you had for redesigning Kitty Johnson's party dress was the smartest thing he ever heard. That's something now, isn't it? But it won't be for long if you go flying off to the next state, will it?"

What was it she'd told Wayne? It was the sleeves, she'd said she'd cut the sleeves off altogether so the pink fur trim around the neckline was the straps for the bodice of the dress, and the fur would set off the soft white shoulders of the lady, who might be Kitty Alice, and might be someone else, maybe someone a little older, a little more sophisticated, which is what a dress like that called for. "Like who, for example?" Wayne had asked her. "Oh, nobody in particular," Lorna answered as she put his hand inside her teal-blue sweater and pressed his fingers into her shoulder.

"Wayne's nothing much to stick around for, Tig, nothing much at all," Lorna's mother said.

"I don't see you ducking his path when he comes to the house for Lorna," her father went on. "Still, I suppose if he's really interested, he'll be here when you come home."

When you come home, when you come home. Her father's words rattle over and over in Lorna's head, each word spit out by a squeal of the brakes as the train pulls into the station. The windows of the passenger cars are streaked with soot. One window frames a little girl with a mass of black hair. She is waving the way only children can wave, like if she waves hard enough somebody will wave back. The conductor stands on the platform with his cap in one hand, jangling a bunch of keys with the other. "All aboard, young lady. Help you with your bag?" he says, as he puts his cap back on and reaches his hand toward Lorna.

"Yes, sir," Lorna says, smiling brightly at the man, her valise midway between them weighing more than a year and a day. And then, "No, sir," she says, and she clutches her valise to her chest, "I changed my mind." Amid the morning mist, the train pulls out of the station.

41

*   *   *

"I changed my mind," Lorna says, pulling the car door closed and setting her valise on her lap.

Her father nods his head. He takes two Lucky Strikes out of the package on the dashboard and gives one to Lorna. She fishes a book of matches from her purse and lights their cigarettes. "Nothing wrong with changing your mind," he says.

Lorna lets go a long sigh, like something that waited for the right moment to fly. Through the car window, she sees a few shoots of grass alongside the road and some skunk cabbage swelling among the trees in the black-earthed woods, hardly enough green to make it seem like April. Still, everything looks so welcome, as though she's been away for ages and come back to the place she loves. Lorna sets her red hat on top of her valise, draws long and deep on her cigarette, and lets the smoke out of her mouth slowly so it makes a swirling cloud around her head.

"Well, Lorna," her father says when he stops for a red light. He pats her hand a couple of times. "I got some errands to do in town. You want to go with me or you want me to drop you off at home?"

Lorna remembers how carefully she made her bed that morning, how she touched the clean white curtains at the window, and dusted the top of her bureau. "I guess I'll just go home." Then she adds, "I got to call Darla."

"What are you going to tell her?"

"I don't know."

42

They ride by Theresa Sherman's shop. Theresa is sweeping the walk in front of the storefront. She waves them over, her hand flitting like a crazy bird come to rest on her hip as Lorna rolls down her window. "I thought you was on your way to Roanoke," she says, as she nods to Mr. Mitchell.

"I changed my mind," Lorna says, "and if you're still interested in having me in your shop permanent full-time, I'd like to come in Monday and talk it over with you."

"Well, I declare," Theresa says. She leans in closer to Lorna. "Don't make any sense to pass up a good thing for you don't know what. Smart girl. You stay here a while, get yourself some experience, you'll have a lot more to offer when you're ready to make your move."

"Theresa Sherman, I got a whole lot to offer right now. You remember that when I come in Monday." Lorna nods to her father. "Me and Daddy got to get going. Is that Mrs. Lloyd in there under the dryer? Don't let her fry too long." She rolls her window up and waves to Theresa.

Her father gives a little laugh as he drives away. " 'Nother cigarette?" He taps out one for each of them. Lorna hopes her father doesn't notice her hand shaking as she holds a lit match to his cigarette.

A lazy drizzle dots the windshield. "New wiper blades, that's something I ought to tend to," Mr. Mitchell says. He pokes his head from side to side, seeing the road between streaks of mud that stripe his view. The drizzle turns to a steadier rain and the window clears until an oil delivery truck passing the other way splatters their car with muddy water,

43

dirt, and gravel. "Repaving this road wouldn't hurt none either," her father says. " 'Course, most folks don't have as much invested in this stretch of road as us. Say, what's this coming barreling our way?" he asks. He bends in toward the wheel, his eyes squinting to make out the identity of the big black car headed toward them. It passes too fast for Lorna to be sure, but she knows it's the truth when her father says, "Looked like the Johnson limousine to me."

Lorna checks the clock on the dashboard. Eleven-fifty. She tries to remember what Wayne said he did Saturday mornings, or to imagine, because maybe he never said.

Lorna's father snaps his fingers and says, "Must have been Wayne come to say good-bye, probably just missed you." He pulls the car alongside the front porch. "You run on inside. I got to check something in the garage." The rain has churned itself into a storm. Small twigs and bits of dead leaves are dancing circles in the air. Lorna holds her hat to her head as she runs up the steps.

The air is acrid with the smell of burnt biscuits as Lorna lets herself in the front door. She sets her hat and valise on the hall seat and walks into the kitchen, her hands first on her hips, then clasped behind her waist, and then crossed over her chest. Her mother is sitting at the kitchen table reading a magazine. "Mother," Lorna begins.

"What on earth?" her mother interrupts. She makes a grand sweep of the table with her hand, scattering crumbs across the floor. "Did you miss your train? You left in plenty of time. I don't see how you could have been late. Honest to God, Lorna."

Lorna stands at the sink and looks out the window. A half dozen pairs of boxer shorts and undershirts are flapping wildly on the clothesline. Lorna turns on her heel and glares at her mother. "I changed my mind."

"Well, I don't see how you can be so casual about something we all put so much work into, Darla down in Roanoke, so many people expecting you." She closes her magazine and drums her fingers on the glossy cover. "Exactly what made you decide not to go?"

"I can't say, exactly," Lorna answers as she drops her hands to her sides. "It was just a feeling."

"Just a feeling? It's got to be more than that." Lorna's mother carefully folds her hands on the table in front of her like she's trying hard to show some patience. "Were you afraid? Is it leaving home that's got you worried, and the going to live among so many strangers? You're so good at making friends, I know Roanoke would feel like home to you in no time."

"No," Lorna says, "I don't think I'm afraid. I'm just not ready."

Her father stomps his feet on the mat in the mud room as her mother stands to face Lorna across the dimly lit room, her curlered and kerchiefed head shaking back and forth. "So, young lady, exactly what do you plan to do? If you're going to stay on here, you got to start paying rent. I'm not going to

45

have a grown woman, child of mine or not, living in this house and not sharing the bills."

"Belle, ease up on the girl," Lorna's father says as he opens the door and comes into the kitchen. "We get by without her money. Let her catch her breath." He strikes a match on the gas burner, lights a cigarette, and pours himself a cup of coffee from the pot warming on the stove. "It's Saturday. I'd like some peace and quiet around here. Your girl being home is no cause for a fuss."

Lorna looks from her father to her mother and then takes her valise to her room upstairs. Through the open windows the wind is whipping the white curtains against each other. She pulls the windows closed and sits down on the chair by her desk, holding her valise in her arms and rocking from side to side.

Lorna stuffs cotton around Mrs. Garber's ears and ties the pink net at the back of her neck. "Pick out a magazine, there's a new *McCall's,* and let's set you up to dry." She fixes the temperature and the timer and steps one dryer to her left to see if Mrs. Jessup's done. "Another couple of minutes," she says as she pats Mrs. Jessup's net back into place.

The telephone rings. Theresa is halfway through a body wave and throws her hands up in helplessness. "Beautiful Hair. This is Lorna Mitchell speaking."

"Lorna, this is your mother. Can you pick up a quart of milk on your way home? Your father forgot and I'm baking macaroni and cheese tomorrow."

"Okay." Lorna is holding the phone between her head and shoulder and pushing her cuticles back while she talks. "I might be a little late tonight. You and Daddy go ahead and don't wait supper for me."

"No buses after seven on Friday. How're you getting home?"

"I'm not sure, I think I have a ride."

"Well, who . . ."

"Oh, there's the bell. Mrs. Jessup is scarlet, Mama. I have to run. I'll see you tonight."

Theresa joins Lorna at the desk. "Who's riding you home tonight, Lorna Mitchell?" she asks. "Here I am, working side by side with you day after day and you don't tell me you got someone waiting for you Friday night."

"It isn't anybody, really," Lorna says. "And I'll probably end up walking. But I like to get my mother to where she isn't so damned sure of my comings and goings." She walks back to the dryers and tilts Mrs. Jessup's hood back. "You must be about done, Mrs. Jessup. Why don't we comb you out?"

Mrs. Jessup moves to the big vinyl chair in front of the mirror. She taps her foot to the tune on the radio while Lorna unfurls her auburn shoulder-length hair from the rollers. She runs her fingers through Mrs. Jessup's hair, which glistens with Lorna's special egg yolk treatment. "You have beautiful hair, Mrs. Jessup, a crowning glory."

"Thank you, Lorna. I'm lucky that way. But I know it always looks its best when you've had your hands on it."

"Will Mr. Jessup be coming to pick you up?"

47

"No, Mr. Jessup's in Wheeling for the day. With Mr. Johnson. Mr. Johnson was kind enough to lend me his car and driver this afternoon. Wayne will be by for me at five-thirty. You know Wayne Lucas, don't you? I understand he's a great friend of your mother's." Mrs. Jessup reaches down to pull her sagging hose up just above her knees.

Lorna ignores the sudden dry feeling in her mouth as she smiles into the mirror at Mrs. Jessup. "How about some hair spray?" she asks.

"Well, just a touch. You know I don't care for it, but if you think—Isn't that Wayne pulled up in front? Will you run out and say I'll just be a few minutes?"

Lorna walks with a brisk and businesslike step. She leans halfway out the door and shouts through the closed windows of the limousine, "Mrs. Jessup will be out in a little while, Wayne."

The passenger window of the black limousine sinks into the car door and Wayne calls to her, "Hey, Lorna, I heard you'd come back from Roanoke. Been meaning to come by and see how you're doing."

Lorna steps outside the shop, closing the door behind her and grips her hands behind her back. "I never went to Roanoke, Wayne. I've been here all along and I'm doing fine." She remembers to smile. "How've you been?"

"I've been fine, just fine. We ought to take one of our rides one of these days," he says.

Lorna recalls the soft gray upholstery of the Cadillac, the smell of Wayne's hair, the roughness of his cheek against hers, how her belly rolled till she feared it might burst every time they kissed. "That'd be real nice. I've got to get back inside. Bye-bye." The late-afternoon sun is blistering. She lets herself back into the shop. It feels cool, even cold inside.

Lorna waves the can of hair spray around Mrs. Jessup's head like she's casting a spell. A shower of sweet-smelling droplets fall twinkling onto the perfect pageboy. "That ought to do it," Lorna says. She prompts the curling hair one more time with a cupped hand. "You want to keep your regular time for next Friday afternoon?"

"Please, Lorna." Mrs. Jessup stands up and gives her hair a pat. "Have yourself a nice weekend," she says. "See you next week, Theresa."

Theresa is reading the Saturday schedule over Lorna's shoulder. "Busy day tomorrow," she says. "If I didn't have this body wave to comb out, I could go home now."

"Why don't you go on, then?" Lorna says. "I'm not in such a hurry to leave. When Mrs. Garber and Mrs. Newton are through I'll comb them out and then I'll close up."

"Well, I surely am not going to say no to an offer like that. I don't usually have Friday nights with Charlie and there's nothing like getting an early start." Theresa collects her belongings and calls to Lorna from the door, "See you in the morning."

Mrs. Garber lifts the hood of her dryer and walks herself back to the chair where Theresa set her hair. Lorna comes to her side, smiling, and spends a long time fussing over Mrs. Garber's very fine, limp brown hair, teasing the top in back to

give the plain woman some height. Mrs. Garber leaves with
a grateful smile. The body wave is a little tight but Mrs.
Newton says she's pleased. Lorna sees her out the door and
locks it behind her.

There's just a few combs and scissors to throw into the
sterilizer, and the sweeping to do. Frank Sinatra is singing
"I've Got You Under My Skin" on the radio. Lorna turns the
volume up and sweeps the soft clouds of brown, gray, and
blond hair toward the waste can near the back door, her hip
pressing against the pole, her face brushing the top of the
handle. She closes her eyes and hums the refrain.

A voice only a few feet away frightens her. She drops the
broom as she opens her eyes to see Wayne Lucas standing
almost by her side. "Your shade was down, so I tried around
back. Mrs. Jessup sent me to give you a ride home. Would you
like me to wait in the car?"

Lorna is flustered and embarrassed. "How thoughtful of
Mrs. Jessup. I'm just about finished. It's nice and cool inside
here; if you don't mind waiting, I won't be a minute." The
broom pole is resting awkwardly on Lorna's foot and Frank
Sinatra's voice is reaching up under her ribs, poking at her
heart. "Would you like to sit down?" she asks Wayne and
points to a chair by the door.

Wayne answers politely, "I think I'll wait out by the car.
It's cooling off."

Lorna empties the dustpan into the waste can. She takes
her purse from the appointment desk, turns off the lights and
the radio and closes the back door behind her. Coming around

50

the side of the building, she wipes a fine band of sweat from above her top lip and smooths her hair back with the palm of her hand.

"Should I sit in the front or the back?" Lorna asks Wayne playfully.

He answers, "I have to get back to pick up Mrs. Johnson in less than an hour."

Lorna eases herself into the front seat. "Thank you for waiting," she says.

"Don't mention it." They ride the couple of miles to the Mitchells' in near silence. Wayne is driving fast, his eyes steady on the road they both know like the lumps in their beds. "Too much air for you?" he asks, as if he has suddenly remembered he isn't in the car alone.

"Not at all," Lorna answers. She's counting on her fingers every time she has seen Wayne Lucas in the past few months, saying to herself which times he was nice and which times he was like a stranger. There's no sense to it except for the truth, which feels more senseless than all the rest and therefore cannot be true at all.

Wayne stops the car at the foot of the Mitchells' drive. "Mind if I let you off here?"

"No, this is fine. Thanks for the lift. Thank Mrs. Jessup for me if you get the chance." She gets out of the car and leans into the window at a polite distance, but before she can say another word, Wayne winks at her and drives away. As she walks up the pebbled driveway, Lorna sees her mother watching from the dining-room window.

The glass in the back door rattles shut behind Lorna. The kitchen is hot and steamy from cooking and closed windows and there's a pile of dishes in the sink. Lorna helps herself to a plate of pot roast and vegetables from the stove. She nods her head at the large box of elbow macaroni on top of the refrigerator in recollection of the quart of milk she forgot. Her full plate is heavy in her hand and she has no appetite.

For Lorna and Theresa, the Friday afternoon of Fourth of July weekend is a blur of flips, pixie cuts, and frosted streaks. Theresa invites Lorna to her house to get dressed for the VFW dance. "No reason to go all the way out to your place when I'm just across the street," she says, as they prepare to leave. "And anyway, Charlie signed on for holiday work and I'm on my own till Sunday morning, so I'd like the company."

They walk the half block to the red-brick house, third in a row of at least a dozen identical houses. Theresa grabs a cold beer and a couple of glasses from the kitchen and they go out to the brick patio in back. A couple of houses away, somebody is playing chopsticks on the piano, over and over again. "I wish Carol Grau would get her girl some piano lessons. Another summer of listening to chopsticks and I might kill somebody." Theresa laughs at herself and looks to see if Lorna is laughing too. "Girl, this is a holiday weekend, one of the only times all year when I close the shop on a Saturday. What in the name of Jesus do I have to do to get you to relax? You've been quiet, but angry quiet, and worrisome as a busy woman can be all day. I know you've got problems at home, and the truth is, as long as you do your work it's none of my business, but I hate to see you like this."

Lorna moves her lips toward something she hopes will pass for a smile. "Relax is exactly what I'm going to do, Theresa, and don't you worry about being meddlesome. Let's you and me have us one more beer. Then I think I'll have a shower, if that's okay with you. That will wake me up."

Theresa goes into the house for the beer and comes back out with a transistor radio under her arm. "If I got to listen to music, it's going to be something I want to hear," she says.

The shattering roar of firecrackers startles Lorna and she drops her glass. The foaming beer spills off a large piece of flagstone and seeps into the ground. The glass lies neatly in two pieces on the wet stone. "Oh, Theresa, I'm so sorry. I'll buy you another one on Monday."

"Don't worry about the glass. Let's go put you in the shower and see if that doesn't help. You're so jumpy." Theresa turns off the radio. Cindy Grau is still playing chopsticks. Lorna and Theresa look at each other and burst out laughing. "Thatta girl," Theresa says, and she pats Lorna on her back.

The VFW is red, white, and blue with streamers strung across the ceiling making a Fourth of July canopy and big bunches of balloons tied to door handles and lamps bobbing in swollen clusters. There's already a good-sized crowd, more than half of them on the dance floor jumping and swinging to "Jambalaya." A visitor from up near White Sulfur Springs asks Theresa to dance just as the band goes into "Love Letters in the Sand." The girl singer wraps her arms around the

53

microphone and makes her eyes heavy, dreamy. Lorna looks at each man in the band, wondering which one of them the girl is singing about. Somebody turns off half the lights, a guy near Lorna hollers, "It's too early for that stuff," and the girls on the dance floor pull a little closer to their partners.

In the half-light of slow dancing, Lorna stands with her arms folded across her chest and lets her eyes wander about the room. "Sure is a good turnout," her father says, coming up behind her.

"Well, if it isn't Tig Mitchell at a dance," Lorna teases her father. "Where's Mom?"

"Oh, she's around here somewhere. You too proud to dance with your dad?" he asks, and he puts his hand out to Lorna.

"I'd be honored," she answers. Lorna's father dances with an unfamiliar kind of formality, but his sure hand is warm and dry around Lorna's waist. She looks over his shoulder at the girls and men nearby, and then to the people lining the dance floor, naming them and moving on to the next face, the next pair of eyebrows, the next set of flashing teeth. And back to the dance floor, looking, searching. Until finally she catches sight of Wayne and her mother dancing in the corner near the exit door to one side of the stage.

In the next moment, the lights come up and the lead singer takes the band into an Everly Brothers song. Now the room is moving fast. Lorna's father draws apart from her, his hand still at her waist. "I bet you never saw me cutting the rug," he says as he twirls Lorna under his arm and draws her into a double-time jitterbug. Lorna can hardly keep up with him.

Other dancers are forming a circle around the two of them, clapping to the beat of "Wake Up, Little Susie" and cheering.

In the second of a series of at least five turns under her father's arm, Lorna sees her mother and Wayne parting. With the next turn, she sees her mother walking to the exit near where they were dancing and Wayne crossing to the exit on the other side of the stage. In the blur of the fourth and fifth turns, Lorna watches them leave the hall. She grips her father's hand tightly to keep her own from shaking. "I've got to catch my breath," she says.

"You mean I'm wearing you out?" he asks. He slows down to where he can turn her under his arm in a graceful flourish to end their dance and let the song finish without them. He leads Lorna to the refreshment table, smiling and waving at the people who call their names as they pass. "You feeling okay, Lorna? You look kind of pale."

"I'll be fine. I just need some air. I'm going to take my pop and sit outside for a while. I'll see you a little later." She turns toward the big open doors at the main entrance. "Thanks for the dance, Dad."

Lorna sits on a long-nosed Impala, sipping her Orange Crush from the bottle. Homemade fireworks rise and fall over the treetops that surround the parking lot, their shimmering light streaking the sky, their whistling sounds cutting the night. The heat from the hood of the Chevy moves up her cold, damp hands and slowly warms her. Lorna lies back against the windshield of the car and cradles her head in her arm.

The music from the dance sounds far away, as though it were coming from across a lake. Lorna remembers a dance up at Summersville Lake the August after she started high school. She was standing on the porch of the lodge with her mother, leaning over the railing and watching the moon rise above the water. They were standing close, hip to hip, moving gently to the music, kidding each other about the boys who were sitting on the steps smoking cigarettes, looking sharp, looking like they were really something. Her mother laughed at them and made them out to be fools. Then the oldest of them, probably not more than eighteen, tall and good-looking, he came right up and asked Lorna to dance. "She's too young for you," her mother said, "but if you put on a shirt and tie tomorrow night, you can dance with me." The boy said he'd hold her to it, and then he walked off. Lorna's mother said it was the greatest joke, wasn't it funny, and she laughed some more. Lorna remembers the sound of her mother's laughter.

But now it isn't the memory of her mother's laughter she hears. One lane away, right next to Theresa's old Ford, is the Johnsons' black limousine. The engine is idling, the lights are on, and the windows are down. Belle Mitchell is leaning on the door on the driver's side, laughing and talking, her voice soft and feathery like a fluttering dove. Lorna half walks, half stumbles back to the VFW the long way around to stay clear of Wayne and her mother.

Inside, she looks for her father, or Theresa, someone. The room is crowded now, steamy with the heat of the night and the dancing. The band is packing up. Somebody is playing forty-fives. Theresa is dancing with the lead guitarist. There's no sign of her father. Lorna wanders out the front door. Her parents are standing on the steps. Her father is lighting a cigarette for her mother, the match is trembling in his hand. "I'll have one of those," Lorna says. She takes a Lucky from the pack in his shirt pocket and a light from the match he holds up to her. Little sparks fly from the straying threads of tobacco. "Where've you been all night," she says, drawing deep on the cigarette and turning her head slowly to face her mother, "Belle?"

"I was just thinking the same thing about you, Lorna Mitchell."

Her father shifts his feet and digs his hand a little deeper into his pocket.

"Everybody knows where I was, dancing with Daddy." Lorna backs up a couple of steps. "Come to think of it, everybody knows where you were too."

Her mother says, "Is that so?"

Lorna is quick to meet her. "Where on earth do you get your gumption?"

"Okay, now, easy there, Lorna," her father cuts in. His cigarette is pressed firmly between his lips and his eyes are screwed up tight to keep the smoke out of them. Lorna looks at her father in disbelief. "How can you—" she begins but he cuts in, "You heard me now, Lorna."

Lorna jumps at a quick and deafening sound, the volley of firecrackers at the back of the lot, and then the shouts of a half dozen boys and the squeals of their girlfriends. People are coming out of the dance hall in a stream. Theresa calls out to Lorna across the crowd, "I'm going out for a beer with some of the guys in the band. Why don't you come?"

Lorna looks from her father to the parking lot. Flashing fireworks light up a hundred cars, and one long black Cadillac limousine parked at the entrance a hundred feet away. "I'm coming," Lorna calls to Theresa. "Wait for me." As she runs to join Theresa, Lorna glances over her shoulder to see her mother brushing the hair back from her father's forehead.

There is no bulb in the gooseneck lamp on the platform at the train station, but there's enough daylight to read the wooden sign painted black and white, with BLUEFIELD in large block letters and the faded schedule tacked to the board by the station-house door. Theresa follows her finger down the columns till she gets to "Saturdays, Sundays and Holidays" and then across the line of dots to "6:17 A.M." She looks above the door to the waiting room at the big clock, which is stopped at 8:25. Then she looks across the tracks to the wall of the valley still in the night shadows of July 3. The tops of the hills and sawed-off mountains are silhouetted in an early gold. Theresa brushes the chipped paint from a length of the railing below the schedule. Then she leans back against it and sets her eyes to the west. "I think I need glasses."

Lorna is sitting on her valise, worrying a straw purse in her lap. "You don't look like you need glasses," she says with a broad and generous smile. "You see everything you want to see."

"And a lot I'd just as soon not," Theresa adds. "You keep on picking at that purse, by the time you get to Roanoke it's going to fall to pieces. You'll have to walk through the train station with all your things in your skirt and won't you be a sight?"

Lorna sets her purse down next to her valise on the wooden platform and stands. "I'm a lot more worried about how wrinkled this skirt is going to be. I'm thinking about standing all the way." She winks at Theresa as she gives a sharp swipe to the blue-and-white-striped gathers of her skirt. "You won't forget to call Darla, will you? Tell her I'm on my way. Tell her what time I get in. Ask her could she meet me at the station or leave me a note on her door where to find her or the key or something. Tell her to leave me something."

"I promise you I'll do everything short of going to Roanoke to see Darla in person," and Theresa points her finger hard, like she's putting a big period at the end of the sentence. "I am so thirsty I'd give a year of my life for something to drink."

"You don't have to wait here with me, Theresa." Lorna takes her friend's hand and squeezes it. "Why don't you go on home? I'll be fine."

Theresa looks for some trace of a lie in Lorna's face. "To tell you the truth, if I don't drink something soon, I'm going to get real irritable." She throws her arms around Lorna. "For God's sake, girl, take care of yourself. Call me if you get into any kind of trouble. When you get yourself situated, I'll be down to see you."

Lorna's head pitches forward in the beginning of a sentence

59

but she can't even get the first word out. She raises her hand in front of her chest and waves at Theresa.

"Don't you worry about things here," Theresa says over her shoulder, already halfway to her car. "Just give it a little time and it won't none of it seem so important."

Lorna hears the sound of the gravel flying out from under the wheels of Theresa's sedan. Every now and then a car passes by and Lorna looks to see if it is long and black and shiny, but the beat-up old wagon and the bright-blue pickup pass the station without slowing down. There is a pay telephone on a post near the road. Lorna fingers the dime in the pocket of her skirt.

The sound of the train is not even a sound yet, just a feeling. A dark-green Plymouth pulls up next to the station to let off a man wearing an old suit and a broad maroon tie. The man leans into the car to shake hands with the driver. The train has just come into sight. Lorna takes her purse and valise and walks to the center of the platform. As the train pulls up, the man in the suit calls good-bye to the Plymouth, straightens his tie, and mounts the steps. There is no conductor to help Lorna. She heaves her valise onto the train and reaches for the narrow iron railing to steady herself up the four steep steps. The man in the suit pushes past her and into the car. As the train pulls out of the station, the BLUEFIELD sign shines so brightly Lorna has to look away.

The Miracle

My sister, Ruby, walks with the step of a giant along the path beside the Naugatuck River. She swings the large bottle of Terpinhydrate with great sweeps of her arm like she is ringing a bell, angry to be going home from the market with no treat, only a pocketful of onions stolen from a foolish farmer, no pretty picture, no story, no dream. When she is angry she looks less than twelve, seven I think.

Oh, Ruby, why do you wear yourself out? The old lady asks a dollar for her saints and martyrs, shiny little cards bright with the halos and tears of holiness, precious golden medals of protection and blessing stitched on purple satin ribbon. These belong to the old lady, Ruby. So what if you want one?

Who told you things would be the way you wanted them? In this life, we must learn to be grateful for what we have and expect nothing more. It is in the market as it is in the home. You call Solange and the Babu mother and father. Beautiful Solange, she is like a child herself, delicate and frail. And the Babu, he is the great destroyer who comes when you least want him, stays when there is no room, leaves when you need him most. For me, there is only one mother and father, the Blessed Virgin Mary and the Lord Jesus. The rosary is my salvation, not the senseless names of mortals.

"I'm hungry, Marina," Ruby says. She is picking at the label on the amber glass bottle and shooting the little shreds of paper at invisible targets, which are everywhere. "If the Babu was home, he'd take us for spaghetti and meatballs," she says.

If the Babu, if the Babu. If the Babu was home, we would hide in the stairwell, reading the sounds of the night with our noses and our eyelashes, listening with our skin for the end of the siege. If the Babu was home, we would be afraid to go home at all until we heard from miles away his big laugh, which moves everything about and sets it back down in the wrong place. "We'll go next door," I say. "Luz will make us something to eat. There is always bread and garlic and oil and maybe some leaves of cilantro like little green feathers," I say, tickling Ruby under her chin, "there is always something."

Ruby tosses my hand from her with an impatient nod and walks with her head down, kicking at swirls of sand flooded from the river only yesterday in a late spring storm. She is always kicking at something. Luz has put long strips of black tape around the toes of her shoes to make them last the summer. "Where did you get that tape?" I asked her. She scratched her head with the pencil she keeps behind her ear, buried in the thick yellow coils of her bleached hair. "A man came to me once with a question. He couldn't pay me. I said I would take something else, something from his red box. He gave me the tape and a special tool, *unas tenazas,* pliers. I use the *tenazas* to turn off the cold water when the drip makes me crazy. This is the first time I ever use the tape. It works very good, I think."

The sun is setting behind the smokestack of the brick-works. Cars passing over the bridge up the river are like the shiny crabs Luz says cover the beach near Havana at night in the spring. A boy on a bicycle passes too close to us. I jump out of his way. Ruby calls after him, "Son of a bitch," in a voice which is bigger than my ears. Then she takes my hand and squeezes it gently. Her hand is bigger than mine and she is half a head taller than me, though I myself am three years older, nearly sixteen. The Babu says that American children grow tallest of all children. Growing up in France may have kept me small, but Luz says I am better for it, that Americans strain themselves by growing so big. Only the Europeans and the Latins know this, and I am European.

We are on the street of three alleys now, five blocks from our apartment. Here I make my arm very strong to pull Ruby past these dark narrow streets so she will not see what may be there, where the buildings look like they will fall in on each

63

other and the cobbled paths break your ankles when you run. A tall man with a shaved head and big pants is standing with a beautiful woman against the front of a building in the middle of the block. They are kissing hard, pushing their whole faces together. He is holding her against him, with the skirt of her green dress gathered in his hands like a rag. She wraps her leg around his hip. I pretend to walk by them very fast and try not to turn my head, but my eyes go so far and then they pull my head around. After we pass, Ruby spits at them over her shoulder. One block from our building she grabs me around the waist and throws me against a truck. She mashes her face against mine, mashes her teeth against my lips, and makes a circle with her hips pressed against me. Then she throws her head back and screams, "Ay, ay, ay, ay, ay!"

"You are mad, Ruby," I tell her, *"tu es fou."* She makes her face very serious, like she is worried that maybe it is true. Then she opens wide her very wide mouth and laughs the pretend laugh, but soon it is the real laugh and I laugh too. Yesterday, when I knelt before the shrine of Saint Anne in the courtyard of the church, I saw Ruby's face shining with laughter in the flame of a candle. Then a big wind broke the flame and her face became twisted, her mouth huge with horror. It is not enough that I see and know of the sadness of life, I must imagine things even worse. I pinched my eyes with my fingers, asked sweet Saint Anne to cleanse my mind of such useless sights and put a penny in the poor box.

At our corner, I hear the rattle of a window going up, and then the voice of Solange: "What could you be doing all this time, Ruby, Marina? Come up this very minute before I die of loneliness." Ruby stands perfectly still and begins to click her teeth like a pair of castanets. Then she puts her right hand flat against her belly and her left hand out to her side, and with her very big feet she begins to take the little flirting steps of the merengue, which is the dance of the Babu. My part is the part of Solange, to sing the song which goes with the dance, "*Dime cuando tu vendras, dime cuando, cuando, cuando.*" Tell me when you will come, tell me when, when, when. The Babu says to make the dance very small and the music very big. In this way he shows off the voice of Solange, which, he tells everyone as he rolls his beautiful blue eyes, is as good as classically trained. Because Ruby cannot sing, and because she does nothing small, she does not agree with this style, so we make the dance very big and the music very small.

On the fifth-floor landing, the door to Luz's apartment, number 52, is open wide as usual. The record player is at the very end of a Julius LaRosa record, which is scratched and warped, but irreplaceable, Luz has explained. She smiles at me from the kitchen table and says, "*Mi querida.*" "*Mi amor,*" she says to Ruby, with a look of fiery passion and then a wink of her big right eye. Her left eye is small, not in actual size but in appearance. A fight with a demon split open the lid and the brow above this left eye. It was swollen shut for days, blue and purple, and then yellow as the swelling went down. When most of the tenderness had gone away, Luz drew fine lines of color around the eye, jade, amber, gold, till this half of her face looked like some crazy peacock. The eye never

65

opened all the way, even after the healing was done. Luz says it stays small to keep the demon out. Ruby swore that one day she would avenge Luz. Luz grabbed Ruby by the shoulders and made her grow still. Then she said, "You will, Rubia," and Ruby's body fell against Luz and they were quiet together.

Solange calls from behind the door of apartment 53, "Ruby, Marina, I am waiting."

Solange is always waiting. Even when the thing for which she has been waiting happens, there is something else to wait for, the morning, the night, spring. Yesterday, she said to Ruby, "I can hardly wait for your hair to be just two inches longer. Then I will make beautiful curls for you, like a waterfall, or tied with a ribbon on the top of your head like a crown." This morning she said, "I have waited long enough. We must cut your hair. You haven't the face for long hair and it is always dirty."

Tonight Solange is waiting for the Babu to come home. This is the best thing to wait for, because he can be gone for a very long time, without a call or a card. This time he has been away only five days.

In the apartment is the thick smell of cigarettes, closed windows, and sleep, but especially cigarettes. It fills the rooms like a dozen woolen coats hanging from the lamps and spread on the walls. Solange laughs when I try to smoke with her. She says I cough like an old crow. Ruby says she has sworn to Luz never to use cigarettes, which make you empty your soul when you exhale, leaving room for the devil to fill you up. After I smoke with Solange I pray to be forgiven. She is less lonely when I smoke with her.

She takes the cough syrup from Ruby and sips from the bottle. "I have been waiting for you, Ruby," she says, "to read to me the comic strips from the Sunday papers. Please start with 'Brenda Starr.' "

For dinner there is a piece of meat Solange has cooked this afternoon. The Babu has said it is impossible for a French-woman to be such a bad cook. Maybe it is because she doesn't eat that she cooks so bad. Still, I take a bite or two and tell her how tasty it is. I will eat later with Luz. Ruby complains about the meat like an old man. She is the Babu when he is gone. But she eats several pieces, and a dish of the noodles and gravy. She will also eat with me and Luz after Solange falls asleep. Solange says we will have fish tomorrow, for Good Friday, and chicken on Sunday after Mass. Ruby says she is going to Hartford on Sunday with Luz to visit Luz's Thursday man, Victor. Solange looks at me for the nod of my head that says, "Of course I will go with you to Mass," and of course I shake my head.

After the meal, we all lie on the couch and watch television, the last half of a very good Western with Randolph Scott, who Solange says is the kind of man she hopes we will marry someday.

Ruby asks, "What kind of man is he?"

Solange says, "Tall," sipping more syrup from the bottle.

"They have lots of tall men in California," Ruby says. "I want to go to California."

67

"It is a long way to California, Ruby," Solange says, "and it costs so much money to get there."

Ruby sits on the back of the couch with her feet on the cushion. "I'll ask the Babu for the money," Ruby says. "He'll give me as much as I need."

"*Mais, qu'est-ce-que tu pense?*" Solange says softly. Her eyelids are growing heavy.

"Speak English," Ruby snaps at her.

"*Mais, qu'est-ce-que tu pense?*" she says again. "What are you thinking? The Babu has no money for trips to California."

"I'll make the money myself then," Ruby says. "Luz will show me how to make the money. I don't need you or the Babu. Luz will go with me to California."

"But understand, *mon coeur*, he must save all his money to build up his business," Solange says. "One day, all of us will go back to live in Paris, that is what the money is for." She stares at the wall between two windows. Ruby makes a growling sound that turns into these words, "Paris, California, Paris, California." Over and over she says them until she trips on one of the *California*'s and breaks out into a cry, "Caw, caw, caw, caw." Solange covers her ears with her hands.

When Ruby starts to beat the pillows with her feet in time to the cawing, Solange says, "Please, Marina, *mon Dieu*, stop her, make her quiet." Her hands are trembling in her lap but her eyes are like black glass.

Ruby's sounds and movements soften. Solange rises from the couch in slow motion and walks in her sleep across the room to smoke cigarettes and file her nails at the kitchen

table. Then I hear her throw open cupboard doors looking for
what she knows is not there and swearing in French. I collect
many days of newspapers into a bundle, which I tie the way
I learned from Reynaldo, Luz's Wednesday man, every bundle wrapped in a cross of thick string. Ruby beats on the back
of the couch with an empty ashtray while she studies from
her lap a map of California in the fourth grade social studies
book which she stole from the school.

Around nine o'clock a man comes to the door. He says he
is a friend of the Babu's. His name is Nathan. Nathan is
skinny and bald, with nervous eyes that look in every direction at once, as though he has done wrong or expects someone
else to. He tells Solange they were introduced at the wedding
of Vita and George. He has just come from the Bronx and he
has a message from the Babu. "Would you like to sit down?"
Solange asks. He takes a seat at the kitchen table. She offers
him a drink. He says he will have rum and orange juice.
Solange says, "I have no orange juice," and pours a glass of
dark rum over ice for each of them. She takes a long drink
from the glass and makes a little face until she has swallowed
because she does not like the taste of rum. Then she draws
one of her long cigarettes from the pack and he takes a lighter
from the pocket of his trousers. She touches his hand as he
lights her cigarette. He stirs his drink with his finger. Solange
calls to Ruby, "Please, you must turn the television down."
She drinks again from her glass. After they sit quietly for
some time, she asks Nathan, "What is the message from
Bernard?" The Babu allows only Solange to use this name.

Nathan wipes the corners of his dry mouth with his handkerchief. "He's on his way home and he'll be very happy to see
you," he says. "He also says to make yourself beautiful"—this
makes Nathan yet more nervous and he looks at his feet—
"because he's got plenty of what you want." He puts his
handkerchief away and stands up, straightening the cuff of
his jacket with a tug. "Thanks for the drink," he says.

Solange gives a small nod of her head and says to me,
"Marina, please show Nathan to the door." I believe it is this
way of hers, elegant even in such a place as the River Arms,
apartment number 53, which made the Babu love her.
Nathan waits while I walk the five steps to the door. "Thank
you very much for coming," Solange says.

When the door is closed behind Nathan, Solange says to
me, "Please, Marina, bring me the little mirror from the
bathroom and my makeup. And if there is a candle somewhere, bring that too."

I pass through the living room, where Ruby is kneeling
before the television, switching from channel to channel. The
shadows on her face change with each turn of the dial, so that
one moment her eyes look dark and her face looks old and
tired, and the next her eyes are bright and sparkling, her
cheeks high and full.

"Who was the visitor?" she asks.

"Someone sent by the Babu, to say he is on his way home,"
I say to her from the bathroom.

"I knew he would come tonight," Ruby calls to me with a
laugh in her voice.

"The Babu is always coming home," I say. "As soon as he leaves, he's already on his way home, Ruby, and as soon as he leaves, Solange is getting ready for his homecoming."

"He sent word. He's on his way," she says as I pass her again with the cracked round mirror on the silver stand and Solange's makeup in a little bag of cotton lace. "I'm going to ask him to take me out to dinner," Ruby shouts from the living room, "all of us, Luz too, and then I'm going to ask him to send me to California."

"Place the mirror here," Solange says as she reaches for the makeup. "And go ask Luz to give you a candle." I do whatever she asks. I go wherever she tells me. I care nothing for myself, only for her. The Virgin tells me I must have pity on her. She has lost faith.

The door to apartment 52 is closed. I knock and turn the knob at the same time. Luz calls out to me from the bathroom, "Do you have any hot water? I want to feel the tropics and there is no hot water. I will kill someone if he does not get me hot water."

From the doorway to the bathroom I say to her, "How did you know it was me and not some stranger at your door?"

Luz looks at me over her shoulder from where she is kneeling on the floor by the tub. She is wearing an old turquoise kimono out of which fall her large dark-skinned breasts like perfect juice-filled melons. Among women, Luz is never one to hide her body. Ruby and I watch her dress nearly every night and rub lanolin on her back and her elbows. "Marina," she says to me, with her hand on her hip and her eyebrow raised with great arrogance, "could you know me all this time and ask such a question? No, of course not. So tell me, do you have hot water?"

"I don't know." I test the hot water at the bathroom sink. "It's true. The hot water is cold."

"So, I will make my own tropics," she says. "Go to the kitchen and light the gas, Marina."

To light the oven in Luz's stove you must have perfect timing and faith in the Lord Jesus. First you turn on the broiler and when you hear the hiss, you light a match, count to five, and reach your arm into the darkness and pray. When the ring of little blue lights has popped up you are safe.

Luz comes into the kitchen with a stack of large pots from the hall. "I will boil my own water," she says as she turns on the tap. "Here, help me to lift this onto the stove, and light all four of the burners." When four pots of water are set on the stove Luz says to me, "So, you came just in time to help me. Go now, and come back later with Ruby and we will eat something."

I turn to leave and then I remember my errand. "Luz, do you have a candle? Solange sent me for a candle."

"Oh," she says, "I have no hot water and you have no electricity." She thinks this is a good joke and laughs at herself. "There, look in the drawer by the refrigerator."

While I sort through the mess in the drawer—a tangle of rope, a light bulb, rumpled papers, a Spanish-English dictionary, a jumbo package of Juicy Fruit gum, a dozen clothespins—Luz sits on a chair and rubs her right foot with medicine from a small green jar which smells like mint and mothballs mixed together. "Here, I have another sign," she says. "I do a terrible injury to my toe by walking into the leg of a table, which only one minute before was not in this place. It is the demon again, who is too busy to come to my house, but sends word that he has not forgotten me."

At the very back of the drawer I find a votive candle in a small glass. "Here's one," I say.

"Good, you have what you need," Luz says. "For what does Solange need this candle?"

"I don't know," I say. "A friend of the Babu came to the apartment to say the Babu is on his way home. Then Solange asks for the candle."

"For this?" Luz asks. "For the Babu she wants the candle?" She grabs it from my hand. "Gasoline and a box of matches, this is what she needs, to burn the house down and leave no trace of herself and be gone before he comes." Her eyes grow narrow and she bares her teeth and spits into the votive glass. "Here, take this to Solange. Go away, go." She turns to face the mirror above the sink. From the door, I hear her say, "So, I am right. The demon has not forgotten me. But I remember, too. *Ven, mal de la noche.*"

Luz is too wild. Sometimes, I wish I did not love her. I pray for her in church. When I told her I light candles for her, she looked deep into my eyes and said she burned candles with greater power than all the little white tapers burning in all the churches in Watertown.

Solange is still at the table, with little pencils and tubes and

73

bottles spread around her, but she is sitting with her head on her arm, crying and speaking in French. Ruby is standing beside her. "Marina, please, what is she saying?" Ruby asks.

I listen carefully to Solange's slurred French, the words spoken between sobs. *"Fini, je suis fini. C'est fini. Je suis fini."*

"She says she is finished, it's finished, these two things, over and over again," I tell Ruby. "What happened?"

"Nothing happened. I came when I heard her crying," Ruby says. "She was looking at herself in the mirror." Ruby grabs Solange by the shoulders. "Sit up," she says, "Solange, sit up and tell us what's wrong."

Solange quiets herself then. "It is this face," she says, pointing to her cheek and sipping from a full glass of rum. "I try with the makeup to cover the marks. Last time before Bernard went away, we had the fight. These little places, you know how we fight, he doesn't mean to hurt me. But he gets angry when he sees them, and we fight again. *Mes enfants, je suis fini."*

I put my finger to the place on Solange's cheek, which has only the shadow of the Babu's hand on it still. I remember the morning he left. Ruby and I stayed the night with Luz and woke to hear Solange calling for us through the wall. Luz opened the big eye to say to us, "Go to her," and rolled over to sleep the rest of the morning. Inside our apartment, Solange sat with the curtains drawn tight, no lamp lit, a hand towel filled with ice to her face. "Please, Marina, *chérie,* please pour me just a little drink. There is some vermouth," she said.

Ruby took the towel from Solange's face and at the sight of the darkness on her cheek, spat on the floor in disgust and threw the towel in Solange's lap.

Now Ruby is pacing the kitchen, kicking at balls of pink dust and small pieces of food. "Please, Ruby," Solange cries, "please, break nothing. It is not so bad. It is only his sadness that makes him so unhappy. It will be good. You'll see. We'll turn off the lights. I'll burn candles. Marina, where are the candles?"

"There is only this one," I say, handing her the little candle, "this is all Luz has."

"We must find more," Solange says. At first there is great fear on her face, but then comes the calculation. "Ruby, Marina, go to the neighbors, knock on every door. Ask them, please, if you can have some candles, all their candles. Go quickly." She lights the one votive candle and sets it by the mirror, turning her head from side to side, tilting her chin up and down, watching the light play on her face.

Ruby stomps out of the apartment and into number 52. I hear the radio very loud, it is Luz's Spanish station. I see Ruby. She sits alone in the dark listening to the announcer who sells furniture, televisions, and cars on credit between love songs, and in the next room Luz is with Victor. What is the use of my perpetual prayer? My eyes are not my own. Now I see Ruby cleaning the dirt under her fingernails with a knife she finds lying on the floor. Then she cuts small nicks from the seat of her chair. She tests the edge of the blade with her thumb and runs the blade against the smooth skin of her

75

arm. As she presses the knife against her wrist, the blade gathers the skin in tiny wrinkles. I press the heels of my hands into my eyes till my eyeballs are twirling bullets and my head is filled with terrible color, angry mouths of green and purple flicking their tongues at me. I implore the Blessed Virgin Mary to save me from the evil within me. What good is there in rosaries and candles when my sight is plagued by such wickedness? Solange is applying blue eye shadow. "Hurry, Marina, please," she says.

I go down to the first floor to begin the search. Three apartments have no candles, no one is home in two others. That is as far as I get when through the shattered glass of the front door I see a black car pull up. I sit and watch from the bottom of the steps as two men get out and stand talking alongside the car. One of them is the Babu. I know him from his black overcoat with the very big shoulders and the long fur collar. I do not know the other man. They shake hands and the other man gets into the car and drives away.

The taps on the heels of the Babu's pointy black shoes click on the walk to our building. He pushes the door open with one of the shoes. "Rina," he calls to me. I cross to him with the timid steps of a child. He takes both my hands in his and kisses the tips of my fingers. "And what is my very beautiful, very French daughter doing sitting in the hall at this hour of the night?" With his thick fingers he gives a yank to the little golden earrings I wear.

I imagine on my neck the warm, wet heat of my own blood trickling from my ears. "I am looking for candles," I say.

"To light my way up the stairs? You are too French," he says, "too romantic." He loosens the knot of the silk scarf at his throat. *"Tout va bien?"* he asks in his very gruff French.

"Certainly"—I speak through the smile I have learned from Solange, the useless smile which goes with the bruises and the days of crying—"of course everything is fine."

"Good," he says as he starts up the stairs. "It's important that everything is fine tonight. I have a little business to do in town, and then we're all getting out of here, we're going far away, the four of us."

"Going where?" I ask. Already he is on the second floor, the click of his taps ringing in the halls in perfect rhythm because his feet never miss a step. "When are we leaving? What about Luz? It is Holy Week," I call to the echo of his footsteps. "Where will I go to church?"

My lips stumble through a voiceless prayer, feeble lips nibbling at words of supplication: I ask Him to be near, at the windows, at the door, or to send His shepherd, an angel, to send something.

"Ruby, let me have a piece of bread. Luz, please, come and eat with us." Ruby tears a piece of bread for herself and passes me the loaf. I have a familiar not-knowing: I cannot tell if I am starving or filled up with fear.

Luz speaks from behind the bedroom door. "Yes, don't eat everything. I have an appetite. That Victor talks like a grandmother. I am just looking in the mirror." She opens the door and steps into the kitchen. "Tell me, do you think I am

77

getting too fat? Victor says I am gaining weight. I don't think so."

Ruby says, "Turn around," and after Luz has shown us her front and back sides, Ruby says, "Now turn around again." Luz turns once more, very slowly this time, looking down at her stomach and over her shoulder at her rear end. "Can I see the backside again?" Ruby says.

"No, you cannot see the backside again. You have seen the backside too much already." Luz moves one of the big pots of water and turns the gas up. "Never mind. If Victor is right and I am too fat for him, there are other men who will like me better this way. Marina, take the pot of chicken from the refrigerator. We will finish it now, and read the bones to know the truth."

"I know what the bones will tell," I say, surprising myself with my own daring.

"You are so smart," Luz teases, "so tell us."

I close my eyes and spread my fingers before me like a blind girl reading a story in Braille. I draw a deep breath. "They will tell that you will grow big like a mountain and wild like the sea and all the birds will nest in your hair." I open my eyes to see Luz and Ruby nodding their heads at each other.

"I did not know you had such a talent," Luz says. "Go on. What more?"

I close my eyes again and touch my brow with the tips of my fingers. "They will tell that Ruby is a thief who has stolen not only onions but also the bottle for Solange from the drugstore"—my heart is beating in my throat so that it is impossible to swallow—"and saved the money from Solange for her trip to California."

Ruby slams her fist down on the table. The salt and pepper shakers, a blue vase filled with plastic purple flowers, a Spanish magazine, all jump like Mexican jumping beans.

"Is this true?" Luz asks Ruby.

Ruby bares her teeth at me and growls. "True? True? What does it mean, true? Did I take the syrup? Yes. Did I pay for it? No. Will I save the money for California?" She rises from her chair and walks the distance to the bedroom and back, pacing. Then she looks at me and Luz very seriously and says, "I'm not ashamed."

"So, how much money have you saved, you who are not ashamed?" Luz asks her.

"It's none of your business," Ruby answers.

"Oh," Luz says, "it's none of my business. Since when is anything none of my business?" She is smiling now. Ruby stands by the table and taps her foot on the floor. "I just want to know," Luz says, "in case I need to borrow some."

This pleases Ruby. "You just let me know how much you need," she says.

"So, Marina, you are very knowledgeable," Luz says, turning to me. "What else will the bones tell?"

I am beyond breath, I speak with my eyes open, my voice is like a tissue passing between my lips. "The bones will say that the Babu, this very night, is taking his wife and children very far away."

"Far away where?" she asks.

79

"She's making this up," Ruby says, as she puts the pot of chicken on the stove.

"No," I tell them, "it is the truth. This the Babu told me, only an hour ago: 'I have a little business to do in town, and then we're all going far away' "—here I look at Luz—" 'the four of us.' "

"Going away, to what, to your deaths?" Luz asks. "This must be a very bad joke, *chicas*," she says, and she pats first my head and then Ruby's.

There is a sound from next door, like something falling, a chair I think, and then the voice of Solange saying, "Bernard, Bernard." We look at one another and wait for more, but there is nothing. Luz takes the lid off the pot and puts her face in to smell. She stirs the chicken and the vegetables slowly, tracing a circle on the bottom of the pot with a long wooden spoon. Again we hear Solange's voice calling the Babu. This time he replies, "Tonight, Solange, get yourself ready," and then the sound of the door closing.

Luz walks from the kitchen to her bedroom and closes the door behind her. Ruby and I sit silently, listening to the little sobs from Solange through the wall. When Luz comes back into the kitchen she says, "So, we will forget the chicken. I lose my appetite." She puts the pot back into the refrigerator. Then she begins to wash the many cups and dishes in the sink. Ruby picks up a magazine from the floor and turns the pages. Luz hands me a dish towel.

"There is hot water now?" I ask.

"Yes, there is hot water now because now it is very important to have the hot water," she says.

"Luz," Ruby says, "I'm here to eat. If you're going to start housecleaning, I'm leaving."

"You are going nowhere, Rubia," Luz says. "There is work for you. The broom is in the living room. Sweep under the bed and in the corners too. And save the dust. Put it in a cup. When you are through we'll eat."

Ruby goes into the living room and puts on the television. Then she comes back into the kitchen holding the broom high in the air. "This is your broom?" she asks Luz. The long green plastic pole has only the stubs of many plastic bristles at the end.

Luz looks up from the sink and gives a laugh. "My Reynaldo is a Fuller Brush man. He is bringing me a catalog this week. Soon I will have a new broom and a mop. Tonight, use this one."

Ruby goes back to her job. *"Ay, caramba,"* she says in a very good Spanish, *"me hace falta un milagro."*

"Sí, un milagro," Luz says, *"vamos a hacer un milagro."* She looks at me. Her face is calm like I have seen it only two or maybe three times before. "We will make a miracle," she says, looking at me.

"The clean apartment is a miracle," I say with the little toothed smile of a frightened monkey. I do not like the stories she tells about what she has done before in Havana, the roof that fell, the broken leg of the mule, the bride whose lover

81

jumped into the sea on his way to the church. The power to
make things happen is a darkness in the hands of a mortal. I
am reminded by the vigilant Saint Theresa that the power to
see is also a darkness, unless the sighted one turns her vision
toward God. But where shall I look for Him in this world that
quakes with Godlessness?

Luz has finished washing the dishes. She takes the towel
from me. "Marina," she says in the voice which is special for
giving instructions, "I will finish the drying. You must do
something very important." She clears her face like she is
wiping a chalkboard clean. "Go to number 53, go home. Solange will be sleeping. Don't disturb her, be very quiet." She
puts a small wooden bowl in my hand. "Collect these things
and bring them to me in this bowl: five hairs from the collar
of the Babu's coat, ashes from his cigarette—only look for the
Dunhill butts, which are his. A speck of dust from each of the
four corners of the bedroom, from the corners, Marina, pay
close attention. Then go to the bathroom. There take the
blade from his razor, only one he has used, *querida*. And wipe
the rim of the bowl, the toilet, with a page from the newspaper. Fold the page carefully, as I will show you, and bring
it to me with the other things." Luz takes a page from the
magazine and carefully folds each of the corners into the
center, and then folds it in half the long way once and the
short way twice, till the page is a small triangle. "So, repeat
to me all that you must bring back." I say the list to her and
she says, *"Bueno.* And if Solange wakes while you are there?"

She waits for me to answer her. "I don't know," I say.

"Very *bueno*, that's right, you don't know. You know nothing. I will tell you everything. If Solange wakes while you are there, tell her you have come for a cup of milk for me. She will go right back to sleep. Go."

I walk to the door, afraid to turn the knob, to step out into the hall, to walk into our apartment. I press the silver crucifix I wear around my neck into my chest. The eight corners of the cross prick my skin and I press harder.

In the apartment Solange is sleeping on the floor of the kitchen, her head and arms draped over the legs of an overturned chair. Ruby and I will take you home, Solange, to St. Suplice, where your mother and all her mothers bent their knees and bowed their heads and broke their hearts before the Lord's perfect sacrifice. She hears nothing as I move about the apartment.

The Babu's coat is lying on the arm of the couch. I pluck five hairs from the collar, scoop a crust of cigarette ash from the ashtray on the coffee table, and go to the bedroom. From each of the four corners I pinch gritty dust from the floor. In the bathroom, there is no razor anywhere, but the small scissors the Babu uses to trim his mustache are lying on the edge of the sink. The seat of the toilet is up. On the rim there are little yellow spots of wet. I wipe just as Luz told me, and make the folds exactly as she said.

In the kitchen I sit on the floor next to Solange. I call her name and kiss her forehead, her beautiful long neck. Her skin is cool and dry. Her lips move. *"Embrasse-moi,* Bernard," she whispers. Her breath is sickly sweet. Luz says this is the smell of unholiness. There is a tiny cut on her chin and a spot of blood on the collar of her white blouse, which is soiled and wrinkled. I am afraid for her and ashamed, my stomach turns and the burning taste of bile fills my mouth.

Luz has dressed. She is wearing a tight black crepe dress with big sparkling rhinestone earrings and a matching necklace. She has swept her hair up into a chignon and made her eyes very black with eyeliner and mascara. Her feet are bare except for the red polish on her nails. The table is set with three plates, three napkins, three glasses, and a bottle of wine. I hear the water running in the bathroom. "Where is Ruby?" I ask.

Luz is standing in front of the sink drinking a cup of tea. "She is bathing."

"She took a bath this morning," I say.

"Did you get everything?" Luz asks, taking the bowl from my hand.

"Yes. No. There was no razor. I brought the scissors for trimming his mustache." I sit down at the table and play with one of the napkins.

"The scissors are fine," she says. Her face softens and she pulls a chair close to mine and sits with her arm around my shoulder. "You are frightened, *mi chiquita*. It's nothing. You know how crazy I am. Don't worry. Here, drink this cup of tea which I have made just for the two of us." I take the cup of pale yellow tea from her. It is bitter and sweet, with a pool of sugar sitting at the bottom of the cup. "I have put up a pot of rice. I am warming the chicken. I have added the green olives you love. Only look how nice the earrings from William match the necklace from Alberto." She touches her jewelry and poses for me. She draws me to her and I breathe her perfume.

Ruby comes in from the bathroom and sits down in the third chair. "This is the silliest thing I've ever worn," she says, as she drops her elbows on the table and sets her head in her hands.

"Stand up," Luz says. "Show Marina how beautiful you look."

Ruby stands with her hands on the hips of a long white dress. The full sleeves fall from the very edges of her shoulders like magnolia petals and the fine lace overskirt is gathered tightly at her waist. Her hair is still uncombed. Blue-black swirls frame her face and her ice-blue eyes sparkle like stars. Her mouth is twisted with disgust and she rolls her eyes upward as she says, "Luz, this dress is so tight I won't be able to eat a thing. I'm taking it off."

Luz turns Ruby around and opens the buttons at the waist. "So, now you can eat as much as you like." Luz draws Ruby to her and Ruby arches her back and stares into her eyes. Then Luz shakes Ruby once by the shoulders and says, "Sit down and I will serve. Marina, pour the wine."

85

The smell of the chicken fills the kitchen as Luz serves us. She sits down in her chair, puts her napkin in her lap, and closes her eyes. After she mumbles something in Spanish and crosses herself she looks up at us, smiling. "Good appetite, *niñas.*"

How fine Luz's chicken is. The three of us eat slowly, picking every bit of the flesh from the bones. Ruby has only to make one spot of the red sauce on the dress and Luz is up from her chair, sprinkling talcum powder on the spot. She unfastens the back. "So, you will eat bare-chested tonight, like a man. This dress must be perfect." Ruby wipes her face with a napkin and smiles at the sight of her own breasts, small like the breasts of Solange. I have the large breasts of the Babu's mother.

The wine makes the roof of my mouth rough. Luz fills my empty glass and Ruby pushes hers, still half full, toward Luz. "It's enough for you," Luz says to her. "Drink slow, Rubia. Stay calm. Have more chicken." I drink deep from my glass. Little streams of wine spill down my chin and my neck.

I love to watch Ruby eat. I pull my chair nearer to hers and rest my head on the table. She uses her fingers and a piece of bread to scoop up the chicken and olives and little pale pink pearls of rice dripping with sauce. Her lips and fingertips are greasy.

Luz tells the famous story of her mother's chicken. This story is always the same and always new. The last time it was an evil priest. This time it is a vicious neighbor. When the neighbor finishes the chicken, Luz's mother asks her if she enjoyed it. The neighbor says it is the best chicken she has ever eaten. How did she make the chicken taste like that, so rich, with such a strong flavor like wild game? Luz's mother blushes and offers her neighbor a dish of flan. The neighbor accepts graciously and asks if there is coffee. Of course there is coffee, Luz's mother says. They sip their espresso. The neighbor makes a very large belch. Luz's mother says *salud*. Is there any of the chicken left? the neighbor asks. She would like to take even a taste to her daughter who is visiting from the other side of the island. Yes, there is some chicken for the daughter. I am almost falling asleep when Luz says her brother Manuel now comes into the kitchen in great alarm. "Mama, Mama," he cries, "I have looked everywhere for Susita, and she is gone."

"Who is Susita?" Ruby asks.

"*Su perro*," Luz answers, "Manuelito's dog."

With my eyes closed I hear Ruby say, "*You* are a dog, Luz." Ruby howls and barks and then the two of them laugh and hit the table with their hands. My head is spinning faster.

I hear the door to our apartment slammed shut, and then there are loud voices but I cannot understand a thing. Luz's kitchen is instantly silent, and then Ruby and Luz get up from their chairs and guide me to Luz's bed. Someone places a cool wet cloth over my forehead. The window is open and the air of this late-spring night spreads over me. My eyes fill with tears and a sob rolls deep in my throat. At the foot of Luz's bed, three candles burn in tall red glasses. Above the candles, a small wooden crucifix hangs crooked on the wall.

I sink deeper and deeper into the bed. The satin cover and the pillows swell around me, muffling the sound of cars passing on the street, a door closing, a man sneezing one floor below, Luz speaking to Ruby in the next room. My lips and mouth are dry. I roll slowly onto my side and reach for the cup of tea Luz has left for me on the nightstand. It is cold and the taste is more bitter than before. I dip my fingers into the cup to stir the sugar from the bottom, but my face grows red with heat, my head or my stomach is swimming—I cannot tell which—and I have to lie back again. When the breeze has cooled my skin, I lift myself until I am sitting on the edge of the bed. There is tightness like a band of cold steel across my forehead. I reach the door with my foot and push it open. A column of soft yellow light falls into the room, and with it the voices of Ruby and Luz.

They are speaking softly, from the far side of the room. They must be lying together on the couch. Luz is stretched out with her head on the pillow that does not have the big hole in it. Ruby's back is pressed against her, with Luz's arm around her waist. Ruby is speaking. "And while we were in Paris with Solange, the Babu was here with you?"

"*Sí*, yes," Luz says, "all the while Solange is in France he is here with me. I go everywhere with him while he does his business. He is so handsome, like Errol Flynn, with the dark eyes and the mouth of a god. I am crazy in love with him, very young, sixteen, maybe seventeen, and very beautiful. He says I'm good for business, I make things go smooth. He likes that I say no to the thing he sells, the drug, the heroin. We eat at nice places, fancy restaurants. Once or twice we go to a nightclub in New York, he takes me dancing. Sometimes he goes to France for a while. Once he takes me, not to Paris but to Marseilles. Solange thinks he is here in America. He sends

88

me back by myself and takes a train to Paris. You are still a child, his child, with his black hair and his cold blue eyes. He cannot bear to be separated from you. He brings you back with him when you are still very little, and Marina, she stays in Paris with Solange. He brings you back to me."

"So, you are really my mother," Ruby says. There is a moment of near silence, they are cooing, traveling across the night sky on the back of God, leaving me alone with the torture of the angry red candles and the crooked crucifix.

Luz continues her story. "It's like this for years. He goes back and forth. Sometimes he sends Solange to Marseilles to receive a package. She brings it to him here and Marina stays with her grandmother. Solange and me, we are great friends always, because I already love her child and then I fall in love with her as soon as I see her, she is that beautiful, and we are like a family in my heart. I make up my mind she will never know, never have even an idea about me and her Bernard.

"I think I am so clever how I hide it from her. One day I learn who is really clever. She finds Bernard and me together, in the bed. She is half-crazed, crying, pulling at her hair. Bernard carries her back to their apartment and after a while she grows quiet, and after a little while more he comes back to me. 'What are you doing here?' I ask him. 'You must stay with Solange.'

89

"He laughs at me. He lights himself a cigarette and he laughs some more. Then he tells me. 'Luz, it's not me she cries for, it's her friend, it's the heroin she loves.'

"So that is how I learn about Solange and the Babu and the

love between them. For so long, I thought I knew their great passion for each other, but then I learned it was his greed for money and her great weakness. For days, for weeks I am lost, confused. I was in love with them, with my dream of their love, and when I learn the truth, I feel like I have nothing. He gives her the drugs, and is like the keeper of an animal. He is a monster.

"I lose the hunger for him. I lock the door to him, I am sick, I tell him to go away. The more I push him away, the angrier he becomes with Solange. I hear the fighting. I turn up the radio, I sing, I swear, I break furniture, I pray night and day. Still they fight. And when I beg him to stop, he says it is up to me and when I take him back, he will be kind to Solange. I can't do it.

"All the while, the two little girls are growing up in a *pesadilla,* a nightmare. I am praying night and day to be relieved of this terrible burden, because of course I see that it hurts not only Solange but also you and Marina. But when I can no longer resist, that is when he starts to change."

"Who?" Ruby asks.

"The demon, your father," Luz answers.

"You mean the Babu is the one who hurt you?" Ruby asks. Her voice is crackling with fire. She is up from the couch and moving across the room, standing by the doorway to the kitchen. I can hear her breathing. "Tell me what you're saying," she demands.

"In time, I grow stupid and I try to reason with him," Luz begins. "I let him in. I say we can be friends. After all, I explain, we've known each other for so long, we've been through so much together, his children are like my children, his wife is like my sister. I invite him in for a drink."

Luz stops for a minute to breathe. "He is a gentlemen at first, and we talk about old times and the life. He leaves with a polite goodnight. But after it is this way two times, three times, he begins to ask for more, and when I say no he says I am teasing him, and when I say I am not, he says he knows I must miss him and long for him as he longs for me."

Now Luz is walking about the room, the boards of the floor are creaking. But Ruby is still and this is the worst of it. I want to be in the room with them, but now it is this bed which is moving away, traveling at a terrible speed. I drag myself to the floor and lean my head on the edge of the door. "This is when he hits you," Ruby says with a hiss in her voice.

When Luz speaks again, her words are especially clear and deeper than before. "He pushes me," she says, "he pushes my arm from the back of a chair. Another time he pushes my foot out from under me where I stand at the door. He begins to throw me across the room. Usually I land on my feet. From time to time I fall. I think he wants mostly to scare me. I stop letting him in and he breaks the lock. I have the lock fixed and he breaks it again. I leave my door open.

"It goes on like this for months, maybe a year. He is gone for long periods of time. When he comes home, I hear the fighting with Solange. When he goes he leaves her enough to keep her going until he gets back, just enough. Sometimes she is able to use it slowly, to make it last. Other times it is gone in one night, and she is sick and weak and must be taken care of. We take care of her.

"She and I are careful together, hardly speaking at all when he is home, stopping to talk on the landing or in the hall soon after he leaves. As the days go by, we are in your apartment or mine together again, Solange and me, you and Marina. I cook and we watch the television. We talk in three languages and laugh and many nights we sleep on the big bed in their bedroom, all four of us. Even if I have someone here, still I come late at night and we are all together.

"One of the times he comes back he has made bad business and he has nothing for Solange. She goes mad. He gets her drunk to quiet her. When she falls asleep, he comes to me. This is the night of the eye. After that, when I see what he is doing to me, I begin to work on him. I don't want to do this, but I have nothing else. A dead pigeon falls from the sky and lands at his feet. The woman who rents him a room in her house for meeting customers sees a tail on him and says she will call the police. The big buyer who comes from Philadelphia dies of a heart attack across the table from him in a coffee shop. When he tells me of these misfortunes, I tell him I know. He stays away and he leaves me alone."

My head is swimming, my skin has a fetid odor. I pull myself out of the bedroom, along the floor into the kitchen. "Marina, what's wrong?" Ruby says, as she kneels beside me and lifts me into her arms.

"It is the tea," Luz says. "I wanted her to sleep. It will

pass." She is still walking back and forth across the living room with her hands crossed over her chest.

My body begins to convulse. A billowing nausea moves through me and when I cry Ruby's name it sounds like someone else's voice. She helps me to the bathroom. I am sick for a long while. Ruby and Luz hold me, wipe my forehead, help me back to the couch, and cover my shivering body with a blanket.

"Marina, you are feeling better now?" Luz asks, petting my head and patting the collar of my blouse, the cuffs of my sleeves. The two of us are sitting at the table, drinking another tea, clear and without color, the flavor like fresh young grass, sweet and cool. Ruby is pacing the room. Luz blows softly on my neck and face. She kisses my eyebrows and the corners of my eyes.

Ruby is pacing still. "Luz, please, you said you worked on him. You haven't worked enough. There's more to do." She stops by the table and stomps her foot down on the floor. "What can I do? Teach me."

The door to our apartment opens and closes. Our three faces turn toward the door as though our ears hear better when our eyes look in the direction of the sound. Ruby's body tenses. Luz holds her by the wrist. "No, wait. He will be gone in only one minute. Business is good. He has come for another package." It is just as she says—the door opens and closes again and the sound of his footsteps falls on the stairs to the fourth floor. Luz shakes Ruby by the shoulders and grabs her by the chin. *"Tranquilísate,"* she says to my sister in a voice that is half a whisper. When her hand falls from Ruby's face, Ruby stands with perfect calm, and over her is a great stillness.

Luz turns to me. "Go back now to your apartment. Go into the bedroom with Solange. If she is not in the bedroom, help her there. Close the door, and lock it. Do not open the door or leave the room until I call you." I look at Ruby. Without speaking she nods to tell me it is okay. Luz turns my face to her roughly. "Go quickly, Marina," and I leave.

Inside our apartment, Solange is still on the kitchen floor and everything else is as it was, how long ago? An hour? Two hours? "Solange, *Maman, leve-toi,* get up," I say to her. Even after I shake her she does not stir. I kneel at her side and speak in a louder voice, "Solange, you have to get up," and I shake her harder. She opens her eyes halfway but she does not see me. I put her hands around my neck and struggle to stand and bring her to her feet. She makes a deep moaning sound and I feel like I am alone with the last person alive. I drag her through the living room. Her foot catches the corner of a rug and then I am dragging the rug too. The door to the bedroom is open. I throw us both onto the bed with all I have of the breath left me. I grab Solange by the shoulders, my fingers digging into her skin and pressing to her bones. "Help me!" I scream into her face, and again, "Help me, *Maman!*" She is lifeless in my hands and her face is unhearing. I push myself away from her and lie on my back.

At the sound of the door to Luz's apartment opening and

closing, every part of me leaps to attention, and I am seeing and hearing with all of myself: running water, cars, a dog barking, the slap of Luz's bare feet on the cold marble stairs and then on the pavement as she runs into the street, the even breathing of Ruby lying on Luz's bed, her arms crossed over her chest, her eyes closed, Luz's door opening and closing again and the Babu sitting down at that table, drinking hurriedly the last of the wine in the bottom of my glass. I reach for the silver cross and chain at my neck. The metal is cold and lifeless in my hand. My eyes sweep the room in search of some sign of God but the room blurs and I am flying down a long, dark tunnel with nothing to hold me back.

Now things without sound are visible. Even the things with sound can be seen but not heard. Stones and twigs and beer cans sent in a silent tumble down to the river by the scrambling Luz. The chair pushed aside, soundlessly scraping the floor, and Luz's kitchen suddenly immense as the Babu crosses to the bedroom door with the stride of a warrior. When he pulls a shiny knife from the pocket of his loose-fitting trousers, when he enters the bedroom and runs to the foot of the bed, when Ruby's eyes remain closed and he stands above her with the knife raised, when his face cracks in recognition because it is Ruby and not Luz waiting for him, his Ruby with her hair spread around her head like a black halo and her sapphire eyes hidden, when I, voiceless, call out in desperate supplication for God's precious and promised protection and hear only the soundless buzz of eternity, when Luz runs mad between two fires she has set at the edge of the river, when Ruby opens her steel-blue eyes and his body shudders violently and his head throws his tongue from his stinking mouth and his eyes from their bony sockets and a world of gray and green slime drains from his nose and his ears, when the knife, driven by his own hand, finishes its curve in his gut, sinking deep into his gut instead of hers, anywhere but hers, when his blood splatters thick and heavy, when Ruby's eyes close once more and Luz squats between the two fires where the water touches only the red polished tips of her toes, when he doubles over with his hands still gripping the knife and falls to the floor, then there is finally a sound, a shriek of such naked agony that it blots out all other sound, supplication, sacrifice, all other sights, all light, all color, till there is only blackness, dumb and final.

Gone

This morning, I walked into my father's room. It's been empty these three years, but just today I saw the floor and ceiling sagging, the walls bulging and the windows buckling with ghosts, the weight and volume of restless memory. It's Benny's going, it's my son's leaving that's made the rooms of this apartment suddenly crowded with phantoms, asleep for so long, awake now. Already I know what they are, how they play like gleeful children all day and fight over me like vampires at night.

   This is the last night we will have together, Benny and me. In the morning, he is moving across town to live in a little room in the yard of the Watertown Brick Works. Night watchman; he saw the sign hanging from the iron fence. "When did you see it?" I asked him. We were closing up for the night. He was sweeping the floor of the smoke shop and newsstand, I was chewing a Mary Jane and counting the day's receipts. "You saw it today?"

"No, I saw it about a week ago," Benny answered. He swept in rhythmic pairs of strokes, long-short, long-short, long-short, the long strokes to push the pile of dust, gum wrappers and cigarette butts toward the front door, the short ones to empty the bristles of the broom. The kind of job they give to the retarded.

I pushed a handful of dull pennies into a red coin wrapper. "They probably got somebody already. You got to act fast if you see something like that." Benny drove the day's sweepings out onto the sidewalk with a firm shot of the broom, the muscles of his back and shoulders rippling like dancing water beneath his shirt. A boy of sixteen with no light behind his eyes, a Jewish bodybuilder with a neck like a gladiator and a thing for Nat "King" Cole. I called to him a little louder, "Anyway, how come you're in such a hurry to go live over there? How are you going to eat?"

Kicking at an imaginary nothing in the doorway, he answered me with his chin nearly touching his chest, "It's not that I'm in such a hurry. It was just an idea."

It wasn't just an idea. He hadn't been too late. "You want to come over and see the place?" he asked me, as I stood watching him fill paper bags with neatly paired socks and stacks of underwear.

98

I waited for a piece of strawberry taffy to grow soft in my mouth. "No," I said. "What do I have to see it for? You want to go, you go. What do they give you? You got a toilet? You got a sink? You got running water?"

"A bathroom, a kitchen sink, and a little hot plate. A desk with a chair. Plus the bed, and a corner for my weights. It's nice, Ma. You ought to come over and take a look." He folded a half dozen shirts from the closet and placed them in another bag.

"And you got to sit up all night watching the place?" I asked.

"No," Benny said, turning to me, "it's not like that. It's not a guard job. It's just to have somebody there. While I'm working I'm going to be sleeping. Not bad, huh?"

That was three days ago. Maybe it was four. I chew my lip to help my concentration. Four days ago was Sunday. I mark time by Sundays because it's the one day of the week I reserve papers for regular customers. It started out as a favor, my own idea, but it turned out to be popular. People like seeing their names printed neatly in the corner of the paper. Several people even said they'd never seen their names written in such a beautiful hand. One woman insisted over and over that I must have learned penmanship in a Catholic school. "I learned from my mother," I told her, but only the first couple of times, and then I let the woman enjoy herself with her Catholic fantasy of me, Sophie Topilsky, then Sophie Liffschutz, only daughter of Karen, who sculpted in stone and played a reckless piano; Karen, whose cough was a mocking

99

laugh, whose laugh was a song; asthmatic Karen Liffschutz, and Malcolm, Malcolm D. Liffshutz, Malcolm the mystic, the mauler, the molester.

Three days it's been, with Benny doubling his curls and tripling his knee presses because, as he explained to me, sweating through another set of plunges, the shiny metal bar resting on his shoulders like a piece of the temple on Samson's back, he might have to miss a workout or two till he gets settled and he doesn't want to lose ground. He packs a little every night. I follow him from room to room. He takes only what is his, and still every room is shrill with the echo of his going, and his going is already forgotten and remembered again, already a useless and terrible piece of the past that leaves room for little else.

"The sheet"—my mother's voice calling from the room above, what was it she had said? "Malcolm, please, bring me a sheet." She was asking for something to spill her cough into, the blood. Then the opening and closing of doors, the sound of my father's wedding ring scraping the railing as he groped for a hold in the dark stairway, the leaden tread of his descent. What about you, Sophie, waiting on the narrow cot, cold with sweat, damp with fear, a pulse like a hammer between your legs, pounding, demanding, hopeless? What about Sophie?

Sophie Topilsky—I call myself by my full name—Sophie Topilsky, don't *hoch* me. Is that the fat of your back pinched under the weight of your own too-big shoulders, pressed

100

against these yellowing sheets? I can only answer yes. Yes, this is me, my chest and stomach buried under the open pages of the paper, my hands black with the ink of the news, the reports, the cartoons and UPI photos, the endless columns of classified ads, Help Wanted. I live among newspapers: By day I sell them, by night I read them. I am surrounded by current events. Still, I can make little sense of the world. I turn to candy. I love the crinkle of the cellophane wrappers, the names like old friends, Baby Ruth, Milky Way, Sugar Babies.

On the front page of the *Herald* is tonight's article about the space satellite. I read it all. Outside the window, the first star shines faintly, a speck of white gold in the blue sky of twilight. I remember the little girl named Sophie who lay in the grass so close to her father, waiting for such a sight. And how waiting had a smell, his smell, pungent, sharp, and sweet, a smell that made her nose run and her tongue grow thick in her mouth.

I turn my face from the window. On page three the advertisements for summer sales, swimsuits, halter tops, Bermuda shorts, patio furniture. Is $14.95 a good price for an aluminum table with an umbrella?

Enough. I throw the paper to the floor, where it takes its place at the top of what Benny calls my newspaper geology, layer after layer carpeting the room, a newsprint plain, and in some places tilting stacks like Monument Valley columns. Come, I coax myself as I heave my fifty-eight-year-old body onto its side. I am a tired slave of gravity, my heavy thighs and fleshy upper arms always seeking the nearest horizontal surface. The bold red and green plaid of my dress flashes in my eyes like blinking neon.

How he pulled me to him with the power, I was sure, of Almighty God, and moved me across the few inches that separated us like I was as weightless as an angel. In the distance between us young grass, the pebbles and clotted earth thrown from our newly planted garden, a fat-bottomed black ant trudging the same distance with a small bit of apple core, all that was left of my father's nightly ritual, the horn-handled paring knife, the clean handkerchief, coils of shiny red apple skin spiraling into his mouth, into mine, the fruit pungent, sharp, and sweet, the distance always too great, the distance always too small.

I part my lips and bat my tongue against the back of my candy-coated teeth, la-la-la, and up from the place behind my breastbone rumbles the sound of a song. Years ago there were words to the song, words formed through my father's smile, words that played on my upturned face, showered on me from his merciless golden eyes, *"Unter a klein beymele, Zitzen yinglich tzvey."* All the while he was tracing the curl and wave of my infant ear, patting the rim of the downy nameless shoot between my nose and my mouth, knuckling the hollow at the base of my throat. Sophie, stargazer, what could you do?

From Benny's room comes the rattle of a window rising, the static of the radio, the pop of a bottle cap and the fizz of warm soda. Bottles of soda he drinks every day in the shadows in the back of the store: the caramel-colored froth he sucks from the round bottle top, the dance of his swelling Adam's apple in his strong neck, his massive adolescent hands, the thick fingers smearing the condensation along the curves of the bottle, the stripes of his short, damp hair stuck to his temples with dried work sweat, la-la-la. Now the groaning bed frame, his shoes tumbling to the floor, a talk-show radio voice, "Hello, you're on the air."

I strain to hear the caller, lifting my head from the bed, my whole upper body trembling with the effort. The words are muffled, something about an election, something about a candidate, a Jewish candidate, something about Jews. Benny turns the dial, static, and then that voice, "Mona Lisa, Mona Lisa, men have named you." He turns up the volume. I know what comes next: a long, vague swelling in his pants, the butterflies in his stomach, the swelling growing to a familiar shape—like my mother's hand guiding my pen, like my father's hand guiding my perfect, tapered fingers against the flimsy white cotton of his shorts, guiding my hips, now above him, now below—and Benny, drawing each breath from his intestines, gasping, "Mona Lisa."

I grip the top of the iron headboard, crushing the cool molded tubing into my palms until my skin burns and my fingers ache. Sobs like a churning sea roll inside me, choked back by the barbed edges in my fever-scarred throat and the memory of my mother's crying. "Go to her, Papa, please," I begged him. He had only pushed more forcefully against the red floor of the porch and sent us and the swinging love seat in a wider, higher arc, the rusty chain squeaking in my ear,

103

the squeaking always a half note off from the pitch of my mother's shriek, the two sounds as difficult together as the music my father's friend Isaac Rubnitz played on the Victrola in the front room of the house on Queen May Street.

"Stravinsky, Sophie," Mr. Rubnitz said, as he brushed the fine blond hair on my arm with the back of his hand, "a brilliant composer."

More static and then the crack of a baseball bat against the ball, "Looks like a single for Mantle. First hit in this game."

What, I got nothing better to do than lie here listening to a lousy ball game? When I got a cupboard full of Campbell's and an empty stomach? The hours and years on my feet in the shop speak back to me as I ease myself to the floor. I roll my gartered stockings down my calves and flex my short toes. They alone, among all the parts of my body and the features of my face, have hardly changed with age. They are still lined up perfectly, each one squared firmly against its neighbor like ten good soldiers, each nail like a tiny cap. This is the way my mother described them to me when she bathed me in the white tub in the kitchen in Brooklyn. Each toe had a name, but both of the little toes were called Napoleon. "Why," I once asked my mother, "why do they have only one name?"

"Because," my mother answered, "they are both so small they need only one name between them." She laughed, her head thrown back, her perfect, small white teeth gleaming, her face beyond my reach. Then she knelt and kissed each of the little Napoleons. But it ended in a bad coughing spell, and my father came in from the bedroom to send her to lie down. "I'll be all right, Malcolm," she wheezed.

"You should rest," he said. "I'll finish Sophie's bath. The doctor says you shouldn't be near her when you are having a seizure."

"It isn't a seizure," my mother insisted, "it's a . . ." But the horrible grinding in her chest rose again. I stared owl-eyed and stiff-necked at my father, his suspenders pressing against the bare skin of his chest, his immense hands swirling the soap into a lather which covered the long dark hairs on the back of his fingers.

On the shelf in the cabinet above the kitchen sink there are cans of tuna fish, sardines, corned-beef hash, cling peaches and a half dozen different kinds of Campbell's soup. Last night for dinner I mixed chicken rice with vegetable gumbo and Benny made a pot of macaroni and cheese from a box. Tonight I look at the labels of the cans until I come to my favorite, tomato. I stir a cup of milk into the red condensed soup in a pot. The two mix slowly as the temperature rises, the Campbell's red and the Brockton's homogenized white. Small and then larger coral-colored bubbles roll up from the bottom of the pot. The color is like salmon, fresh salmon, which I ate once in a fine restaurant with my father and his new wife, Natalie. Papa ordered fresh oysters and salmon for the three of us. I couldn't get one oyster down my throat, not even after Natalie covered it with horseradish and cocktail sauce, not even after Papa demonstrated with oyster after

105

oyster, sliding each one from the shell into his mouth, sliding one from his mouth into Natalie's purple lipsticked mouth.

The stove top is dotted with cream of tomato. The soup is too hot to eat now. I turn off the gas burner and set the pot in the refrigerator to cool.

Benny calls from his room, "What's for supper?" He leans in the doorway, rubbing his eyes like a sleepy child. "I'm getting hungry."

"I didn't think you wanted anything. I made myself some soup." I open the refrigerator door and test the soup with the tip of my finger. It's just right now. I tuck Sunday's *Parade* supplement under my arm, let myself out the back door, and sit down on the third-floor landing. From the kitchen of a new family on the second floor comes the television broadcast of the baseball game. Someone has hit a home run and the announcer is shouting, "The season's first grand slam! Look at them go!" The voices of too many children, squealing with delight, hurrahing, whistling.

I round my lips and try to whistle. Once, and for a long time, me and my father and mother were famous for our trios, she with her hands dancing among the black and white keys, Papa and me breathing sound. We did Chopin nocturnes and études and passages from the *Scheherazade* Suite. Even after Mama died, me and Papa continued the tradition. Then I was sick. My mother's cough tore at my throat and racked my chest. Natalie went to live in Hartford for the winter and Papa sat beside me, night after night, rubbing liniments and mentholated oils into my chest, sleeping only in the minutes between the eruptions, breathing for both of us when the bed shook with the violence of my coughing. When the illness was over, Natalie came back and Papa closed my bedroom door at night. But if, before morning, he thought he heard me cough, he stood outside my door and listened, and sometimes, even when there was silence, he let himself in. To lie down beside me, lie down behind me, circle my new hips with his strong legs, spread the lips of my sleeping sex with fingers made wet in my uncertain mouth, drive himself into my young darkness and whistle in my ear.

"I'm going to have some cereal, some oatmeal," Benny calls to me through the screen door. "You want some?"

"No," I answer, "it's too hot for oatmeal."

"You're eating hot soup," Benny says, standing with his nose and forehead pressed against the fine mesh, his body outlined in a blurred silhouette behind the screen. "I got some bananas," he adds.

"Okay, make me a little," I say. "You going to eat it in there?"

"Yes, I'm going to sit down here at the table, and sprinkle some sugar over it, and a big pat of butter . . ."

"We only got margarine."

"So a big pat of margarine, and then the sliced bananas and a little milk. I think I'll make some coffee too."

"I don't want coffee. Just a little cereal." I let myself into the house. Benny is standing at the stove stirring the oatmeal, wearing only a pair of khaki-colored pants, no shoes, no socks, no shirt, no undershirt. His belt buckle dangles from the loop of his pants. I set the empty soup pot in the sink and lean toward his back as I move to the table. I can feel the warmth of his young skin. His pants stay up without the belt; though he has his grandfather's narrow hips, he has the full, high fanny of Harry Topilsky. From a chair at the table I say to him, "You look like your father more and more."

"Not like the pictures I've seen of him," Benny answers.

"You can't see everything in the pictures." I go into the living room and return with a silver picture frame, which I set on the table.

"So why do you bring the picture in here," Benny asks, "if you can't see anything from it?"

"No reason, just because I never look at it."

"There's no reason to look at it," Benny says, "no reason even to have it." He sets a bowl of oatmeal on the table in front of me. "You want a little milk?"

"Yes, pour me a little milk. But listen," I say to him, "what is it you got against him?" I turn the photograph toward myself. "You didn't even know him. You never heard a bad word about him from me. How is it you have such a bad feeling about your father?"

Benny puts his supper on the table and stirs milk and sugar into his coffee. He takes a big spoonful of cereal with a slice of banana. He chews slowly. He's thinking. "Grandpa," he says.

"What do you mean, you mean Malcolm, you mean my father? What? Did he say something?"

Benny nods his head while he chews another mouthful. He

swallows and then he trims the edge of his bowl with the spoon. "Yes. Grandpa Malcolm."

"So what did he say?"

"He said there was someone before my father, someone who really loved you, who would have taken good care of you, but you wouldn't have him." He takes another mouthful of cereal.

So unflinching in your evil, Papa, so reckless, with your Tchaikovsky burning out tubes in the radio and rattling the glass of every window in the house, your stomping, slippered feet kicking at chairs, at walls, at doors, while in my room, my husband, Harry, panted—I was someone's wife, Papa— and threw himself despairingly over my senseless body.

"Of course there were other men," I insist to Benny. "I was nearly forty when I married your father. I was thought to be, well, a very attractive woman. But Harry Topilsky was a gentleman. And he was kind."

I am making excuses for the dead. Kind tonight was dull, unthinking, unseeing so many years ago.

The man in the picture is wearing an Air Force uniform, with the cap set back on his head and his hand shielding a high-browed face from the sun. Even with no other soldier to measure him by, you can tell he was a big man, over six feet tall, barrel-chested, but with a hesitancy about him, in the set of his eyes, in the almost-smile. Some things don't show yet, the stoop of his shoulders. Maybe they weren't so rounded then, maybe it was only after the war, after a year or two working with Malcolm Liffshutz, that Harry Topilsky bent

109

his back and shrunk his neck. But Papa must have known those shoulders could round, must have sensed that back could bend. He heard it in Harry's stutter, and saw it in his eyes so ready to tear, a man who could die that fast, choking on the bone of a boiled chicken.

Harry was the last of a dozen men—my father called them boys—soldiers, sailors, an officer or two, a mechanic who was one of two gentiles, the other was a doctor. Eleven young men, and there could have been dozens more, because, Papa said, I was a beautiful woman.

In the bedroom closet, in a box of photographs and newspaper clippings, there is a picture of me wearing a little black hat with a veil, a borrowed fox fur over my arm, and a corsage of roses pinned to the lapel of my suit jacket. Above the photograph, this title: THE BEST-DRESSED WOMAN ON THE BOARDWALK. On that spring day, I walked into the finest tearoom in Atlantic City on the arm of Mr. Samuel Levitsky, a salesman with a good line of well-placed housewares—he sold only to department stores. He was the cousin of a Mrs. Levinson, a wealthy friend of Natalie's mother, one of a large party invited to spend the day taking in the sights and the salt air on the Jersey shore.

After Atlantic City, Mr. Levitsky used to come into the shop for cigars. He liked to stand and talk with Papa while he kept his eye on me. One day when Papa was out, Sam—he said I should call him Sam—he told me he had big dreams for me, because I was gorgeous—that was his word. He pressed himself against me in the back of the store. His breath was heavy with the sour smell of Havana tobacco. He kissed my neck roughly, he buried his face in my breasts, he drove his tongue into the pit of my arm. He told me he could get me into the pictures.

I was foolish. I told my father. "What does a goddamned salesman know about the pictures?" he shouted at me, and I never saw Sam again. Then there were years without a date. I worked, Natalie left, we moved to Connecticut. Then came the war, and the USO, the boys home on leave, and Harry.

"Your cereal's getting cold," Benny says.

"I lost my appetite." I take a toothpick from a little glass I keep on the table and pick at the last of this morning's rye toast, a caraway seed lodged between two of my back teeth. As it turned out, I had the kind of good looks that didn't last. Right after Benny was born my knees started to fall. And that was just the beginning. Not that it matters now. How beautiful do you have to be to sell newspapers and cigarettes? My customers aren't looking for anything but a clean front page. Like Mr. Creely, who shuffles down the stairs from his third-floor apartment above the store to buy the evening paper and torture me. "Is this the only paper left?" he asks every night, examining the print of the paper in his hand.

"No, old man, there's another dozen papers just like it," I tell him, making myself busy emptying cartons of cigarettes and chewing on an occasional stick of licorice. "I order an extra dozen, twelve more than I sell, just to make sure you have a good selection, so that when you go back to your cell and lock your door and pull down the shade you can be sure you have the right paper." What drives people to such lone-liness and isolation?

"I guess it's getting late," Benny says, drinking the last of his coffee.

"It's not so late," I say. "You're so busy?"

He makes a stack of his dishes on the table. "I still got some packing to do," he says.

The clock above the stove says 8:45. It's about three quarters of an hour slow. The black round face with glowing green numbers and hands was a premium I bought from a magazine distributor who tried to sell me on a line of movie and love-story magazines. "This is a newsstand," I explained to him.

"These magazines *are* news, Mrs. Topilsky," he said. He was clear-eyed and clean-cut, the kind of young man who ought to have a regular job, an office, and a lunch hour.

"These magazines are heartache," I told him.

"But heartache is news, Mrs. Topilsky," he insisted.

"Only when you're young," I said. But I took the clock anyway, and the *TV Guide,* eighteen copies a month to start. For every ten copies I sold, I got a quarter back on the price I paid for the clock. I made a couple of bucks back before it started to slow down. I took it across the street to the jeweler to see if I could get it fixed. He said it wasn't worth the price of the repair to fix it. So I brought it home. I figure in about thirteen years, and for maybe a whole day, it will tell exactly the right time.

"You want to take the clock?" I ask Benny.

"It's broken," he says over the rim of his coffee cup. "Anyway, they got a clock there. A big one."

"How are you going to wake up in time to go to school?"

"The gatekeeper said he'd knock on my door," Benny answers.

He's a smart kid. He's got an answer for everything. But he's shy with strangers. It's just me who knows what a good kid he is. I reach across the table and tousle his hair. Young hair. He ducks his head down and lowers his eyes like a shy little girl. "You going to come home and see me once in a while?" I ask him.

"What do I got to come home and see you for?" he asks. "I'm going to see you every day in the store." He puts his dishes in the sink and runs the water. What do I care? He's no company to me. He wipes his face with his wet hand and ducks his head in uncertainty. "Sure, I'll come and see you. We'll fix this place up. Make it nice. I'll bring my friend over."

I reach for another toothpick and upset the glass. "What friend?" I ask, as I pick up the toothpicks and put them back in the glass.

Benny turns the water on a little harder and puts some soap on the sponge. "Maria," he says.

I never saw him wash the dishes before. I know he does it once in a while, when the sink gets full. But I never actually saw it myself. I was always reading the paper. "What Maria?"

He washes each glass and dish with soap and makes a pile

of sudsy things on the counter. "She's just somebody I know," he says.

Now I got a terrific appetite. "What kind of somebody? You got a girlfriend all of a sudden?" I ask as I feed myself a mouthful of cold, tasteless oatmeal.

He turns the hot water on harder to rinse the dishes. "No," he says, "she's just a friend. From school."

The cereal is like papier-mâché in my mouth. I can hardly get it down. "What is she," I ask Benny, "she's Italian? That's an Italian name?"

"I don't know what she is," he says, shaking the water from his hands. "She's Tony DiStassi's sister. Yes, I guess she's Italian."

"So," I say, pushing the empty bowl toward him, "you got a friend. That's very nice. You got a friend, you got a room, you got a clock. Sixteen years old. You're doing very nice for yourself, aren't you?"

"Mom," Benny says, like he's asking me for something, there's a question, an asking in his voice.

"What, Benny, what do you want?" I say to him.

He can't answer me. He puts my bowl in the sink and runs the water again. He braces himself against the counter, his shapely arms straight, the heels of his hands pushing against the trim, his fingers spread like claws. On either side of him are stacks of old newspapers discolored with time, stacks Benny sorts and tends carefully, useless stacks of newspapers he prefers to the random collections in the bathroom, in the hall, Benny's work, his futile pleasure, lifting weights, sweeping the floor, and making stacks.

If I could eat newspapers, I would have a feast, a hundred-thousand-course meal. As it is, I got a lump in my throat the size of a golf ball and a horrible cold sweat covering my body, a cold dying feeling all over me like a rubber sheet. Over my shoulder, behind my eyes, a black and endless hole, and at a distance I cannot measure, Papa grinning at me. Benny dries his hands on the sides of his pants and leaves the kitchen.

"I've been thinking," I say, following him to his room. He's stripping the sheets from his bed and folding them properly. The bed linen he treats like silk. That's how I should have treated him. Then he wouldn't be going away. "I've been thinking I might take in a boarder. An older person, maybe. I hate to see the room empty."

"Sure," Benny says. "Sounds like a great idea. Got anybody in mind?"

I sit myself down on a corner of the bare bed and run my hand over the striped mattress ticking and the buttons. "No, I didn't think that far ahead yet. I thought I'd wait a while. To make sure it's okay, to make sure everything works out for you over there."

He is making a pile by the door, great bars and disks of steel—the toys of a young Atlas—bags of clothes, boxes of papers, odds and ends. "I'm sure it's going to work out," he says. "I was by there today. They cleaned it up nice for me. I got a new lamp by the bed. And a radio."

"You don't need a radio, you got this radio. Here you got the AM and the FM, and with an antenna you could hear broadcasts from Europe, from South America." I unplug the radio and wind the cord.

"They got me a transistor, Ma. It's little. It doesn't take up a lot of room." He puts the old Admiral back on the bureau. "Maybe your boarder will use it."

"You got such a small room you have to worry about the size of a radio?" I unwind the cord and plug it back in. "Never mind, I'm going to do just like you say. I'm going to keep it for my boarder. I think I'll get a new TV set too, a color TV. I'm going to get an RCA Victor with a big screen."

"RCA," he says.

"That's what I said," I say. What's he going to sleep on tonight is the question in my mind.

"No, you said RCA Victor," Benny says. "They don't call it that anymore."

"How come you stripped the bed?" I ask him. "You going to sleep on the bed without any covers? No pillow?"

He checks the drawers of his bureau one more time. He's only moving across town but he's acting like he's going across the country. "No," he says, turning to me. He's still without a shirt. The muscles in his stomach are taut and his hands are tightly fisted at his sides. His father was never this handsome. He's got a waist like a girl, a wasp waist, and skin wrapped around his muscles and bones like a fine jersey, seamless, supple, beautiful like I've never seen before in a boy, a man,

GONE

sixteen, a know-nothing kid, his nipples like crushed pome-
granate seeds.

I stomp my foot on the floor. A welcome pain shoots up
from my heel to my hip. "So where are you going to sleep?" I
say.

"Over there," he answers.

"Over where?" I say. "What are you talking about?"

"Over at my room, at the brick works," he says.

"I thought you were going tomorrow. In the morning." My
mouth is dry. I feel in the pocket of my dress for the Life-
Savers. Butterscotch, they are stuck together. Three of them
fit in my mouth with enough room for my tongue and my
questions. "You're going tonight? How are you going tonight?
I thought we'd have breakfast together in the morning. I was
going to make biscuits. Remember my biscuits? I was going to
make a baked apple."

Benny grabs an undershirt from the top of a bag. "Maria
and Tony are coming over after they finish eating. Tony's got
his father's car. They're going to help me. It works out better
this way." He lifts his arms into the undershirt. For an in-
stant his head disappears inside the blue cotton and he stands
like a faceless god. "They'll be here any minute," he says as
his boy face emerges again.

Benny fills his arms with bulging brown-paper bags and
walks to the kitchen door. When he has brought everything
from his room, I look at all there is of my son's life. It's very
little, it's only enough to fill the backseat of a car. When my

117

father and I moved to Connecticut, when we sold the house in Brooklyn and moved to this Catholic town, we had little more. "Leave it," Papa said, "leave everything. We'll start over." Natalie went back to her mother again—"You don't need a wife," she screamed at him, "you got Sophie"—and Papa and me lived in the little room behind the store, and then the little room above the store, Mr. Creely's room. Every time we moved, we left everything, and every time there was less to leave. But we weren't starting over. There were no new beginnings. There were just the endless piles of newspapers, and every cigarette in the entire universe passing over the counter. Like shadows, they hid the thing between us, because since I was grown, a woman, we didn't know how to be together. He couldn't bring himself to touch me, but I saw how his hand lingered where my body had been, his palm vibrating from the heat my buttocks left where I sat on the edge of a chair. I was nearly his height, and he was alone, and there was no one to love me, no one to challenge him, I was there every day, beside him, behind him, in front of him with my dress riding up the backs of my legs as I bent to tie my shoe. He couldn't bring himself to touch me, and I ached for him, and dreaded the sound of his breathing so near, the beard of two or three days of hopelessness on his falling cheeks.

118

Every day I hung our coats in the closet and ate my meals with him, our muted eyes sunk in the pages of editorials, advertisements, obituaries. And every night, alone in my bed, I dreamed: I set fire to young children and burned the skin off their innocent faces, tore from them their eyelids, their lips, their ears, their genitals. In the morning at breakfast I stirred two spoonfuls of sugar into his tea and folded his napkin just so.

And he brought me candy. Whitman's Samplers, foil-covered hearts, long strings of red and black licorice, yellow-and-orange candy corn, truffles. Customers returning from Paris, from Vienna, brought him candy to give to me, sent him boxes of sugar-coated pears and chocolate-dipped plums from Berlin, from Rome. For me, and they smiled, and imagined that they petted me, purred over me, plotted the use of my used body, imagined the paths he had taken, sucked at my breasts with their eyes. When finally there was Harry, they laughed into their snot-filled handkerchiefs; when Benny was born they made signs of devils and of the cuckold at his *bris,* at his *bris,* do you hear me? Only when Harry died, only then did they hide their faces, a momentary lapse into shame, and call Benny a Topilsky, you could he see was a Topilsky, that was the manhood of a Topilsky, how they never let up. And when Malcolm died—I thought I would go with him, I thought we would go together—they went to their offices, they opened their shops and answered their phones, and not one of them followed me to the cemetery, none of them came to watch him lowered into the ground, no one cared, or needed the assurance that he was really gone, or the promise that even if he changed his mind he had a half ton of earth, of dirt—are you listening, Malcolm?—hundreds of pounds of rock and soil to weigh him down while he lay for eternity with the memory of my wretched delight as his only companion, leaving me with the boy, the bastard child of Harry and Sophie Topilsky, Harry married to a woman forbidden him, Sophie promised and possessed from birth, the boy, Benny, his father's son, his grandfather's curse.

The buzzer, the door. This Maria, and Tony. "Here, children, sit down, a cup of tea. We have tea, don't we, Benny? I'm sorry there are no cookies. DiStassi, what's your father's name? Maria, you sit here. Have a piece of candy. Benny, pass Maria the candy. You like caramels, Maria? In the cupboard I have caramels. Joseph Junior? No, I don't know his name." Oh, she pats his hand, her fingernails pink and white, perfect edges, tender cuticles.

"Well, we better get going," one of them says.

"Sure, sure, I got things to do too. I got to clean up."

"So, I guess I'll see you tomorrow afternoon, Ma," Benny says.

"That's right, tomorrow afternoon." From the landing, Benny turns to wave to me, his herculean arm, his dumb face reaching toward me, he is frightened. I fumble in the pocket of my dress. What became of the lemon drops? The other pocket is empty too. In the kitchen, I search the countertop, the drawers, the cupboards, I scan the floor. Miniature lemon candies, each one the size of a pea. They come from England in a round white tin, a fancy habit.

Sophie, Sophie, such determination. I march methodically from room to room, certain, confident. I will find them. I look: here, in the medicine cabinet; no, there, behind the pillows of the sofa; maybe under yesterday's paper. Finally, of course, where they have always been—we've known each other for decades—in my room, between the mattress and the box spring of my bed. The lemon drops exactly where Papa kept them, kept count of them. Every night he selected one single sun-yellow sweet, placed it delicately between my lips, waited for the citrus perfume to fill my mouth. *Benny.* Pressed my high school lips apart with his skilled fingers. *Is gone.* Laid his father lips against mine, sucked my heart up into my throat, swallowed my breath and my life with one kiss. *Never. A kiss. Not one. Benny is, praise God, and damn Him, gone.*

As Much As I Know

When the light is green and a car passes doing forty-five, I get the feeling of wind passing through a ghost town, nothing to move, nothing to stir. But we are here, Jessie and me, moved and stirred by the wind, not ghosts at all.

My Jessie is nine, but she's got the face of an old lady, mostly around her eyes. The rest she'll outgrow: a big nose, ears that stand out square from the sides of her head, arms and legs long and loose like limp noodles. It's that tired look that worries me. Nothing a bath wouldn't help, though, that and some clean clothes. She's sitting under the picnic table, sorting pebbles and bottle caps and adding carefully to the piles she's collected.

I shoot a handful of her rejects one at a time across the rest stop, aiming for the telephone pole, missing more often than not. What a wild-goose chase this was, going all the way down to Nashville just because some lamebrain says they're hiring at the Oprey, dragging Jessie behind me. What on earth was I thinking? I've got the sense of a fool and the weight of my mother's words bearing down on me heavier than sin.

"Jeannette, are you talking to me?" Jessie asks.

Sometimes I don't know when I'm thinking in my head and when I'm thinking out loud. On the other hand, you live so close with somebody, like a mother and a daughter do, you get to where you know each other's thoughts. "Was I talking to you?" I ask her—now I know I'm talking out loud—"I guess so. To you, to myself, to whoever's passing out favors to whoever hasn't collected one for a while. I sure could use a favor. But right now I'd settle for a cigarette. Roll me a cigarette, Jessie."

She reaches into my jacket pocket with her fingers, long and skinny like chopsticks, and pulls out a tightly wrapped package of Bugle. She spreads some of the rust-colored tobacco on one thin sheet of paper and rolls a perfect cigarette. "Jeannette," she says, handing it to me, "no matches."

"Why didn't you say that before you rolled it?" I say. "Maybe somebody dropped some, talking on the phone. Take a look over there." At the booth she holds up an empty matchbook. "Next driver stops'll have a match or a lighter," I promise.

What else will he have? A story, a flat tire, a job? A place to stay for a couple of days, a wife, a place to stay for a couple of months? A knife, dirty words, regret? For years I've been looking for safety from this unlikely inventory. But it's been too long, and lately with nothing but suspicion and fear for what's coming. It's only caring for Jessie and what's left of my sense of humor that keeps me on my feet. That and the simple fact that I don't know what else to do. But it's gotten to where "don't know" sounds less like an honest reason than an excuse.

At the sound of a car coming, I put my thumb out. It might not be too much longer before we get picked up. We've already been here close to an hour, so it isn't likely that another dozen cars will go by without one of them stopping.

A black '52 Ford pulls onto the shoulder with four people in the car, a lady and a man stiff and unmoving in the front seat, and in the backseat two children. The man gets out to check the water in the radiator. The boy is talking, waving his hands, pointing, and shaking his head yes and then no, answering his own questions. Next to him the girl, a year or two younger than Jessie, is sitting with her back to the boy, gazing out the open window. I watch her eyes leap from the trees to the patches of grass to an empty lot across the way, staring at the place, a stretch of road, a rest stop, like she's committing it to memory. The man screws the cap back on the radiator, closes the hood, takes his seat at the wheel and they're on their way. People with children never pick up hitchhikers, not even hitchhikers with children.

I turn the collar up on my jacket and dig my hands into my pockets.

"You cold?" Jessie asks.

"No," I answer.

"How come you got your collar turned up?" she asks as she climbs onto the tabletop and sits with her knees rubbing against my shoulder.

"Just a habit, I guess. C'mere. We'll turn yours up too." Jessie hums "Mockingbird" and taps her foot on the bench while I fuss with the frayed, lifeless collar. "There. Now you look real sharp."

A pale-green Pontiac squeals to a stop and a red crew cut leans across from the driver's seat. "How far you headed?" he shouts over the radio.

"If that's Chuck Berry I hear, we're going as far as you're going," I answer.

He gets out of the car to open the trunk. "That's Chuck Berry, okay, and I'm going all the way to Scranton," he says. "Let's put everything but the kid and the guitar in the trunk." He smooths the sides of his hair back with the palms of his hands. "On second thought, let's put everything but the guitar in the trunk," he says. He's about my height, maybe an inch or two taller, and he's got freckles and dimples. He loads the trunk and slams it closed. "Let's go, kid," he calls to Jessie.

"Her name's Jessie," I tell him. "Mine's Jeannette."

Two twangy guitars are winding out with "Johnny B. Goode" as he pushes the front seat back for Jessie with a sweep of his arm, like he's welcoming the queen of England.

"I forgot my bottle caps," she says, looking over her shoulder.

125

"They're dirty," I say. "Leave them where they are." She bites her bottom lip and lowers her eyes.

"In you go, Jessie," the redhead says. He slides onto the woven car seat that gives him some height and turns the key. "I'm Tommy Skelton, no relation to Red, and the only thing you have to do is sing when the radio signals get too weak to pull in a good song."

He's got a bag full of little cellophane-wrapped cakes on the backseat. Jessie spots them right away. By the time he says, "Help yourself," she's already halfway through a lemon pie and holding a cinnamon ring with her other hand. "Why don't you offer one to your friend here, if you think you can spare it," he says.

The last thing she ate was a bag of fried pork rinds and that was a good four hours ago, so I don't expect her to be polite. Anyway, he's just teasing her, which is a good sign, because when they're warm to Jessie they're usually pretty decent with me. "I'm her mother," I tell him, "and I don't much care for pie, but I'd like to get a light for my cigarette."

"Matches in the glove compartment," he says.

"You smoke?" I ask him.

"No, I don't, but I love the smell of them." He steps on the accelerator and leans back into his seat. I draw long and deep on the cigarette. It tastes the way cigarettes used to taste—sweet, fruity. The smoke rushes to my chest and my head fills up with a welcome blur. Long rows of elm trees are flapping their branches like banners in the wind. Jessie is sleeping with her mouth open and a half-eaten cake in her hand. I feel a morning of stiffness and dread easing out of my body. I wish to hell Scranton was at the other end of the earth.

Tommy breathes in smoke from my cigarette with a smile. "My mother's kid brother Robert is an artist," he says, as he sinks a little deeper into his seat. "He's only about ten years older than me. The summer I was eleven, he had me up to visit. I stayed with him in his studio in New York. He was doing a bunch of illustrations for some big tobacco company, and he'd have a different beautiful model in the studio every day." He smiles at me. I give him half a smile through the cigarette pressed between my lips.

"Robert let me watch. One day he'd have a blonde stretched out on the floor, wearing a bathing suit and sunglasses and smoking a cigarette. The next day it would be a brunette relaxing on a satin couch reading a magazine, or a redhead brushing her hair while her Pall Mall cigarette burned in a fancy ashtray.

"Sometimes I'd bring the models a glass of water. Lunchtime, I'd run out and get sandwiches for all of us, and at the end of the day, I'd empty the ashtrays. Each cigarette butt would have this bright red or orange or pink lipstick ring around it. I saved one butt from each model and I wrote their names really tiny on them, Cynthia, Kay, Sheila. Every day Robert would ask me at the end of each day if I was in love, if I liked Kay better than Cynthia. I always told him yes, because I thought that was what he wanted to hear, but I never actually preferred one to the other, because I wanted them all."

127

He pauses to look at me, his face set and serious like it might crack if he moved it, freckles and all. Then he goes on, "For years afterward, I dreamed about them, and always the dream was the same"—he sounds like a preacher describing the day of resurrection—"me in Robert's studio on that satin couch with a half dozen beautiful women around me, each one smoking a cigarette, and me breathing in that smoke like it was keeping me alive." He lets out a deep sigh and tightens his hold on the steering wheel. "The truth of it is, I'm a sucker for a pretty girl with a cigarette hanging out of her mouth"—he looks over the back of the seat and nods at my guitar—"but a pretty girl with a cigarette and a guitar might be more than I can resist." He reaches across and lays his cool, damp fingers against the back of my neck. My skin crawls. "Oh, come on," he says as he tightens his grip and pulls me toward him.

I'm thinking about Jessie, wishing she would wake up, then hoping she sleeps through, telling myself this is nothing to worry about, this is something, this is nothing.

I ought to be accustomed to it, ought to expect it, but sometimes it catches me unawares. Tommy is twisting the loose strands of my hair around his hand. I feel a scream building in my throat, a shrill "no," and I hope he doesn't see my eyes filled up with tears.

He loosens his hold and pats me on my arm. "Easy now, girl. Nothing to get upset about. Let's just take it real easy." He brushes the knees of his trousers with a sharp flick of his hand. "Maybe you've forgotten what a good-looking woman you are," he says.

This is what it's like: you're tossed about with fear and flattery, never quite sure how to put them together, never knowing an enemy from an ally. And maybe that's the real danger—that they're usually one and the same, the man who runs his fingers through your hair, or under your blouse, is the same man who may feed you and your child tonight, and tomorrow, and maybe all week. I'm not ashamed to admit I'll go out of my way for anybody who gives me and Jessie a roof over our heads and food on the table. You do things you couldn't imagine doing until you're there, at five o'clock in the morning, sorting rags with a toothless old man in Detroit, sleeping with him on a rag bed every night, comforted by the sound of his snoring—you don't begin to hate it until six weeks have gone by. But the times like these, when you haven't had the chance to figure out just what you can expect from each other in order to have an understanding, they're the hardest of all.

Tommy straightens himself in his seat, rolls down his window, and turns the volume up on the radio. The air is soft and cool on my face. Johnny Mathis is singing "It's Not for Me to Say." Then it's noon and all the radio stations are giving the news. "I'll read it tomorrow in the paper," he says. "Why don't you shut that thing off and sing me something pretty."

The last time a man told me to sing something pretty I spit in his eye. But this morning, singing feels like getting off cheap—somehow I know he's going to leave me alone now. "How about a hymn?" I ask him, mostly joking. He plays along, says he likes a nice hymn, especially unaccompanied. My lips and my mouth feel frozen as I begin "Leaning on the Everlasting Light." Then, after a chorus or two where I'm fighting a big lump in my throat, my voice grows deeper and deeper, a plumb line bound for my belly. Jessie wakes and climbs over the seat into my lap. She presses her cheek against my shoulder and hums into my chest. Tommy breaks out in a whistle with the richest line of harmony I ever heard. As my voice trails off, he softens his whistle to a whisper. In my head it mixes with the lullaby of the turning wheels. My eyes grow heavy and I feel like I'm dreaming, and then I'm dreaming that I'm sleeping and then I'm sleeping.

"Jean," I hear a voice say. I shift in my seat. "Jean, we're almost there."

"Almost where?" I ask.

"Scranton," he says.

There's a stretch of service stations and little restaurants. Then we drive past block after block of frame houses, two-family, four-family, shingle, brick, shaded windows, bare windows, screen doors, open doors. People park their cars, call to a neighbor, shout at the dog. For a while I have that nice funny feeling I sometimes get in a car, when it's like a little room and all of the people in it are separate from everything we are passing, separate and untouchable. Then the separateness is gone and we are vulnerable to all the things outside. Jessie burrows against me. Her weight is a comfort to me, makes me feel rooted in this uprooted life we live.

"Where you headed?" Tommy says as we stop for a red light.

On the street, a man driving a hillbilly car stacked high with crates and boxes, a mattress, and a wringer washer is talking to a boy on a scooter. The boy looks like my brother, Del, or like I remember him, fair and blond, with dark-brown eyes and buckteeth. I can't hear what the boy is saying, but I watch him as he points out a right turn to the driver and counts intersections on his fingers. Asking directions is part and parcel of my life, just like Tommy's question, "Where you headed?" It sounds simple enough, and when I know the answer, it shoots from my mouth like a belch. But when I don't know, when I am not headed anywhere, just someplace that hasn't come to me yet, it's like waiting to grow hungry so I'll know what to eat.

Sometimes, often I guess, I've heard myself practicing inside my head, "Home, we're going home," and it sounds like a prayer to me. I used to believe in prayer. Maybe if I pray from this minute until I walk into my mother and father's house, I won't have to think too much, or wonder if there'll be a place for me, for Jessie, or what it will cost in pain and pride. "I'm not sure," I tell him. "You can set us down anywhere."

Tommy piles our belongings carefully on the curb. "Haven't heard near enough of your singing. Wish I was going

131

farther." He bends down to Jessie's height. "So long, Jessie." He gets back in his car, waves, and pulls away slowly.

I send Jessie into a store for something to drink. It's starting to cloud over and the wind's come up. I ought to pull out another sweater for her. She walks slowly down the steps in front of the store, sucking hard on a straw buried in a small carton of chocolate milk. "I got this from the man inside," she says, handing me a cigarette. "I told him it was for you. I got matches, too."

I put the cigarette and matches inside my package of Bugle. I wonder what time it is. I should have asked Tommy. The guy in the store probably has a clock. Sometimes I'd just as soon die on the spot than have to put my thumb out one more time. I hate like hell always having to ask for something. God, I hate it.

A repairman is working in the store. He's an older guy with a face like puffy dough. He comes out to get some tools from his truck, checks his watch, and looks us over closely. Then he says he's about through for the day, and if we don't get a ride before he's done he can take us twenty-five miles up the road. He leaves the truck open so we can sit inside if it starts to rain.

Jessie's been sniffling and her eyes are glassy, so we set our things in the back of the truck and wait in the cab. She sleeps and I read an old newspaper. The repairman comes out after a while with a Coke and a turkey sandwich. He steers with one hand and eats his lunch with the other. About halfway through the sandwich he says, "Did the little girl eat?"

132

"Yes, she did," I say, "but thank you for asking."

"Ain't it hard on her, traveling this way?" he asks.

Jessie is still sleeping. I brush her hair back from her face. "She does all right," I say.

"Don't seem proper," he says. "A child needs to be in one place."

"She does all right," I say again.

"I guess it's all right," he says, "if you don't know any better." I stare out the window at the Barbasol and Pennzoil billboards. "Raise her like this and she'll end up tramping around when she gets older." He makes a sucking noise through his teeth. "Are you a tramp?" he asks. He snickers through his nose and shakes his head. Men like this are more a bother than a danger, nosing around looking for something dirty and seeing it wherever they look. I am singing "One Hundred Bottles of Beer on the Wall" to myself because it's the longest song I know and it helps me keep my mouth shut and my brain still when I need it.

We don't talk any more, except he gives a snort every now and then. When he pulls up in front of a filling station with a battered old Trailways sign right above the pay phone, I take Jessie in my arms and ease us down to the ground. He slams the door behind me and guns the accelerator in neutral while I unload our things from the back. He leaves a spray of gravel behind him as he drives away.

The guy inside says his name is Steve. He's an olive-skinned man with a lot of muscles and a lot of gut, and he smells like he's been drinking. He tells us to put our things

133

alongside the soda cooler under the awning. Then he invites us to have a seat inside by the electric heater and take the chill off. It sounds like a good idea. I can't keep going if Jessie is getting sick, and she's losing color by the minute. He makes a place for her on a car seat he must have pulled out of a wreck and I throw my jacket over her.

She sleeps for well over four hours. I look at an old *Time* magazine. Steve pumps gas, drinks beer, and reads a parts catalog. He talks to his wife a couple of times on the phone. We don't say much to each other. It's already dark out. The room feels like it's growing smaller and the distance between me and this man is shrinking. He finishes his last beer. "I've got to close pretty soon," he says. "I can't let you sleep in here, but you can stay in the ladies'."

"Thanks," I say.

While he is locking up, I bring our things inside. He follows us around to the back of the building and opens the door to the restroom. It smells like undiluted disinfectant and urine. He turns on the light and stands looking at me while I set Jessie down on the concrete floor. It feels like the smallest room in the world, cold and damp, with a dripping faucet and a running toilet. He takes a halting step into the room, he looks at me again. We are measuring each other and the night and the wind and the darkness. Then he turns and walks away. I watch him get into his car and drive off.

Light comes out of dark so slow it feels timeless, like it was always light. I've been watching through the frosted window above the sink. By daylight, the room looks less dingy, less squalid. It's just the starkest, grimmest place we've ever slept in, nothing more, nothing less. I feel like I'll never be clean again. I tended Jessie only when she cried out. The rest of the time, I tried to forget her, her hunger, her filth, her fever. It's sinful: I've shrunk my shame and learned to ignore her when I have to. But she acts like she knows it, and won't have even the little I give her at those times; the assortment of covers I threw over her, a ratty blanket from a junked van outside, my jacket and sweater, she kicked them all away. She's curled up in a ball in the corner by the door, holding to herself whatever body heat she can muster.

Steve knocks on the restroom door. "I got some hot coffee and some juice for the girl," he says.

"Okay," I say. "We'll be around in a while."

Jessie wakes lightheaded and weak, cries till she wears herself out again. Her nose is running, her lips are dry and cracked. She's dead weight in my arms and her head is leaden where it rests on my shoulder. All of a sudden I begin to weep uncontrollably, saying Jessie's name over and over. She starts crying too, saying, "Ma, Ma," and I promise her right out loud that we will never, ever, spend another night in a place like this. Silently, I pray I am not lying.

The sky is an even gray. The cars and trucks that rumble by sound like a muffled snare drum. A woman climbs down from the cab of a scrap-metal hauler parked in a truck stop across the road. She throws a yellow jacket around her shoulders and waves to the driver, who has started up his engine.

135

She looks across at me as she pulls a yellow chiffon scarf from her purse and covers her head. She ties the ends of the scarf in a big bow under her chin, fussing with the loops till they match perfectly. It starts to rain. The driver toots his horn as he pulls out and the woman walks in the opposite direction, waving at me and Jessie. Jessie waves back.

The coffee is just the way I like it, black and strong. After a couple of gulps I can feel the spaces between my teeth again. Jessie downs the orange juice and asks for more. "I'm going to get you some more," I tell her. She looks at me with doubt. I circle her waist with my hands. "I promise," I say. She shakes herself free and reaches for my coffee.

Steve comes in from waiting on a customer while I'm rolling myself a cigarette. He pulls a box of raisins from a bag by the door, tosses them to Jessie, and tells her to dig in. "Looks like we're in for some nasty weather," he says to me. "You might have to hole up here for a while." He looks fidgety, like he wishes he was half his size. "Listen, you play cards?" he asks me.

"I know canasta," I say.

"I bet a couple of hands will straighten this weather right out," he says. "Give you a chance to win some pocket money."

"What's in it for you?" I ask him.

"Getting rid of you," he says.

"All you have to do is ask me to leave," I tell him.

A car pulls up in front of the pumps. He pushes two decks of cards toward me and grabs a slicker from a hook by the door. "Shuffle and deal," he says on his way out.

Jessie is picking raisins from the carton one at a time, squishing them between her fingers until the skins break and then smearing them on her lips. "You going to share those raisins?" I ask her.

She comes up to my chair and stretches a finger to my face. I part my lips. She pinches them together and coats them thickly with layers of raisins. Then she takes one step back to survey the mess she has made of me. Looking satisfied, she pops a whole raisin in her mouth, chews it thoughtfully, and pops in another. "Mmmm, these are good," I say, licking the sweet paste from my lips.

"You want some more?" she asks.

"Don't mind if I do," I say and peel a few from the carton she offers me.

Jessie retires to a corner of the office and counts the raisins out into her hand, then counts them again as she places them back in the carton. I shuffle the cards. It's a heavy, steady rain now, pelting the roof relentlessly, making little puddles in the gravel lot in front of the station, and I'm glad for cover. The weather is buying me time, just a few hours to get used to the idea of going home. I didn't always want to. There were times like the year I spent frying eggs and flipping flapjacks in a diner in Canton, Ohio. Me and Jessie lived in the little apartment above the diner with a Mexican farm worker named Juan Cruz. Juan bought the place off an old German who just wanted enough money to get to Florida. He wanted to put my name on the deed, said he'd make it half mine, all legal, if I'd stay. I almost did. He was good to us, he taught

Jessie songs in Spanish, and gave me a white lace mantilla for Christmas. In fact, I think I left because I was afraid I might grow to love him and that was somehow more painful than the others. They were what I was used to, the hundred guys like Tommy, a hundred hands reaching out to hold me, the diaper delivery man who jumped me in the back of his truck, and the old black man on the motorcycle who wanted me so bad and cried so hard when I said no that I almost changed my mind. But somehow none of it seems as bad as last night. I am dangerously close to not caring for my child. Else how could I have allowed her to sleep on the floor of a room most people shun, even for the time it takes to drop their drawers? Now that I've made up my mind, I try to remember where I thought I was going, what actual place I was headed for before I decided on home. I can't remember, and can't imagine where I might go if they turn us away.

Steve and me alternate canasta with crazy eights right through the morning. Jessie sleeps on and off, sits in my lap and tells me what cards to play, sleeps some more. I am dealing another hand of canasta when he looks at his watch. "I'm going to open up a can of stew. I got a hot plate in the garage and a roll I brought from home. It's more than I can eat. I only have one dish, but I'll wash off a fork for you." He looks like he could put away a can of stew and more, but I'm too hungry to say no. Jessie won't have the meat, but she'll eat some of the potatoes and carrots. I don't think Steve counted on sharing his lunch with both of us, but I'm way beyond apologizing.

We've been talking all morning about nothing in particular, me asking Steve questions about life in Susquehanna County, him asking me questions about all the places I've been. Over the stew and another hand of canasta, he asks me about my family. "We've lost touch," I answer. He looks like he's going to ask me another question I don't want to answer. I'm sitting with a feeble hand, and I don't need to meld, but I pick up his jack of clubs and the four piddling cards under it.

"Can't say no to those princes, can you?" he says.

"Oh, I've said no to my share of them," I say with a sly arch to my eyebrow.

A car pulls up at the pump and the driver gets out and opens the hood. Steve sets his cards down and says on his way out the door, "You're so far ahead of me I know I can count on you not to cheat."

I've said no to my share of them, that's what I told him, but the truth is there was only one no that ever mattered in all these years, no when I thought I was saying yes. Yes, Teddy. You bet, Teddy. Lord, yes.

Two brothers married two sisters and had a boy and a girl apiece, me and Teddy born in '35, Del and Joyce born a year later. The two families moved from Knoxville to Syracuse right after the war. Our houses were side by side, so close you could hardly ride a bike between them. Everybody said it was perfect that way. Perfect. Holidays, school days, summers, snowstorms, we were like a little army. We shared everything, so we got half as much of whatever came into our house as we would have otherwise, but half of everything they got

139

too. Except somehow me and Teddy found a way to have it all. If Louise made a pie and sent half over to us, I gave Teddy my piece. When my mother knit gloves for everybody and I lost mine the first day I wore them, Teddy gave me his. Everything that came from me he gave back to me. I stopped wearing dresses because we couldn't share them. My mother wanted us all to mark our clothes because she didn't like Teddy's shirts and jeans turning up in our wash. Aunt Louise told Teddy he could play football with Del after two years of saying absolutely no, and we both knew it was because she thought practice would keep him busy, away from me.

We didn't care. I sat in the bleachers and watched him every day. The summer we turned fourteen, Preston and Louise said they didn't want to take the house at the lake for a week like we'd all done every summer for years. They wanted to drive to Cape Cod instead. Teddy got whooping cough in the middle of July and spent the rest of the month in bed and most of August lying in the hammock singing with me. Preston and Louise learned to play golf, my mother watched me and Teddy over the top rims of her glasses, and nobody went anywhere.

Uncle Preston was in a bad accident on the job that fall and Louise had to go to work. Teddy and Joyce ate at our house most of the time. Louise would come over for supper late, after she'd got out of work and stopped by the hospital to visit Preston. Preston kept getting worse. He had one operation, and then another, and then he got some kind of poisoning after the second operation. My mother said it was a nightmare. It was about all everybody talked about, everybody but me and Teddy.

We were busy writing songs and planning our careers, dreaming about our TV show, which would be like *The Jimmy Dean Show,* or like Perry Como, and we would always do duets, or we would do solos but with the one not singing onstage all the time. But that would be only once a month. The rest of the time we would travel around in a big Airstream trailer and see the country, hunting and fishing and doing surprise shows for people in little clubs here and there.

If somebody had asked me why I loved him so, I don't think I could have said. I don't think he could have either. It would have been like trying to say why your hand was at the end of your arm or your eyeballs inside your sockets. But maybe we could have said that it was like breathing, something we knew was a part of us just because we were alive and together in a world of our own. It wasn't till after Preston died that I started to feel guilty for having taken so little notice of what had been going on.

Louise stuck it out for as long as she could by herself, but even with my mother and father's help, it was hard on her. Grandma told her to come back to Knoxville. Teddy and I thought it was a great idea because we thought we'd all go. Louise sold the house and most everything she owned to the Wilmores, packed the rest into her old station wagon, and left in time to send us Christmas presents from Tennessee.

With Teddy gone, I discovered I had no life by myself, and

only one friend. I started going to the Baptist church with Sue Sue Washington, whose brother was the quarterback on the football team. When she joined the choir so did I. They put me in the back row at the far end and I sang with the baritones. I used to watch the women in the front of the sanctuary whipping the air with their arms and wailing to God, singing, "Help me, help me, Jesus." I knew they had something I wanted, so I raised my arms and my voice. They said the choir was no place for a soloist and asked me to leave.

I only saw Teddy one more time, and it was my mother who made it clear it was one time too many. By that spring I was playing my own music and I'd taught myself enough chords not to shame myself on the guitar. I heard about a contest for a record contract in Nashville. I took my guitar and as much money as I could lay my hands on and I got Sue Sue's cousin to drive me out to the highway. My first ride was with a trucker who said the only reason he wasn't going to rape me was because I was jailbait. It was the first time I was glad that I looked as young as I was. He gave me twenty-five dollars and dropped me off at the bus station in Pittsburgh. I bought a bag of potato chips and a Coke, put the rest of the money in my pocket, and hitched all the way to La Follette. I called Teddy and he came and picked me up.

It was only a few months since we'd seen each other, but it could have been ten years for all the growing he'd done, surely four inches taller, his shoulders that much broader than last year's shirts, a beard and the razor burn to go with it, and a different smell, pungent, earthy. Dear Lord, he was

142

gorgeous, and it surprised me in a funny way, as though I'd never noticed before.

We were wild. We hugged and kissed each other over and over and when we got back in the car, I didn't let go of his hand for a minute, not even when he was shifting gears. We drove toward Nashville, talking all the way. And when we weren't talking I sang to him, sang gospel songs, and then my own songs, the love songs I'd written for him, and the fierce and driving songs that were half me and half gospel. His favorite one was "Long Gone Lover." He made me teach it to him the minute he heard it. He especially loved the verse, "Lover, you've been gone so long, / That's why I had to write this song, / Just to tell myself it's true, / There was a time of me and you."

We stopped and got a room in a dumpy little motel near Sparta, nervous as hell, pretending we did this kind of thing every day. We ate some sandwiches and watched TV till every channel went off the air. Teddy went to the bathroom and I turned the lights off and got undressed.

He came to bed wearing everything but his shoes. When he kissed me I pressed my tongue against his lips. I felt his face melt, everything went soft and wet, his eyes were tearing and his nose was running. I think he nearly died from the relief of holding me. It wasn't just the months we'd waited, it was our entire lives.

143

The heat rose off his body in an enormous wave. I started tearing at his clothes and he was tearing at my skin like I was still dressed and then he was naked and me somehow nakeder than before. We fumbled all over each other, our hands were trembling, our bodies shaking. When he came up into me it hurt bad and I cried. I whimpered at first but then I howled and the more I howled the deeper he drove himself inside me, till when he reached his climax and filled me up, I was nearly blinded.

He was breathing hard and heavy on top of me. I was still feeling the fire in my belly and seeing it behind my eyes. Inside me, he was growing small, pulling away. Every part of me was screaming no till it was a roar in my head, and then I was whipping the air with my arms, telling him, saying it, singing it, "No, Lord Jesus, no, please no, please don't stop." Singing it, then chanting it till it was a song, and then it was something else, a telling, till it changed from a no to a yes and he heard me, heard me all night long.

The morning dropped over us like a heavy curtain, darker than the night. I woke from a half sleep. Teddy was pulling on his pants with his back to me. Where was I going and what was I going to do? he asked me, while he stood in front of the bathroom mirror combing his hair. I reminded him about the contest, said how I thought we could go into the city together, maybe find a room someplace. Teddy said he had to get the car back. He'd left a note for his mother, but he knew she'd be worried. He had football practice. Wasn't I coming home with him? I told him I was going to Nashville and please wouldn't he come with me? He just said no, but he'd take me where I was going. Then he told me to be sure and call his mother and come and visit before I left for home. My head was swimming and every time I moved I felt the ache of the night before, like I was carrying a stone between my legs.

Teddy made his way around Nashville real well. He found the address where they were holding the auditions without any trouble. When we said good-bye I thought I was speaking in a foreign language. He hugged me and said he loved me and even that sounded foreign. The only real thing was that his chin was shaking and his spit was thick. I thanked God for giving me at least that much, so I knew he was feeling something, even if he couldn't say it.

I had to wait six full hours before I got to try out for the producers, which was probably the best thing because it took me nearly that long to feel like I was there, and that I was a singer, and that I had a song. While I was waiting my turn, I talked to two girls from Louisville. They played the accordion and the ukulele and sang hit tunes like "A Garden in the Rain." I figured I was probably better than them but they had great outfits, aquamarine mohair sweaters with skirts to match. I thought my tight black skirt and cardigan might hurt me.

But when my turn came, I told myself that talent was all that counted. I sang "Too Bad Love" the way I learned in church, full out and full up. They let me sing it all the way through. There were four judges. One sat with his fingers over his mouth, another with his lips all screwed up. One was biting his nails. When I finished they said they liked it but it wasn't what they were looking for. I asked them why. They said it was too much song for a woman by herself and told me to get a guy to work with.

Their words simmered like sludge in my stomach. I took an especially long time putting my guitar back in its case. Then I walked real slowly across the stage, down the steps, past the judges to the back of the theater. I found my way to the main road north. I don't remember how I got there, only that it took a very long time and I seemed to be going around in circles. I know I was being watched over because it wasn't five minutes I'd been standing by the sign marked LOUISVILLE 138 MILES before a woman trucker hauling a load of tires to Rochester picked me up. She was a talker, but she didn't require that I ask a lot of questions or give my own opinions. She just seemed to like believing that someone was listening, and she didn't need any more evidence of my attention than my body in the cab and my eyes open. She didn't ask me much about myself either, except to wonder how my mother and father might be feeling about my being gone. But I was too taken up with a thousand useless attempts to change my memory of the night I'd spent with Teddy to worry about my family.

I tried to imagine what I could have done that would have made it all different, but even in my dreams it always ended the same way. We always had to kiss, we always had to love, and to lose ourselves in each other that way. Then we had to come apart, farther apart than we'd ever been, probably too far apart to ever be close again. I tried to imagine him at football practice, at the kitchen table with Aunt Louise and

Joyce, and I couldn't find a place for me in all of it. Then I tried to imagine him with me on our TV show, in the Airstream, at the little clubs. But I couldn't find us in those places either, couldn't bring those old stories to life. I felt more alone than I'd ever felt before.

Del was sitting on the porch when I got dropped off at the corner. He was reading the newspaper and eating a banana. I wanted to run to him and let him hold me and knead my back with his knuckles like he did whenever he knew I was feeling blue. But he didn't even wave when I came up the walk. He just shook his head and said, "You're a dead man."

My father gave me unending hell for being away four days without a call and only a stupid damned note that said not to worry, which was stupid because how could they not worry? "Four days," he kept shouting at me over and over again, with the veins at his temples swollen and red and his hands beating the air. He said I better have a good story to explain where I'd been. My mother said there wasn't a story good enough to explain. I figured nothing I said would make any difference so I didn't say a word.

I was confined to the house for the rest of my life. I spent every night and weekend writing letters to Teddy that I always tore up the next day. I could never find the right thing to say that would be like a bridge between us the way we had been together before that night and the way we were afterward.

I didn't admit to myself that I was pregnant until I missed three periods. My mother said she knew right away because there was nothing from me in the waste can in the bathroom. She never asked me what I was going to do or said what she thought I ought to do. She only wanted to know one thing: Had I been to Tennessee the week I was gone? I knew how grave this question was and I answered her straight away, "Yes, ma'am," trying to hold my body still, feeling like my arms and legs and head could go flying off me every which way, breaking furniture and tearing down walls.

She looked at me from behind her silver-rimmed glasses, her face so stern, so set. We were sitting at the kitchen table. It was late in the afternoon. She had a book open in her lap. Every once in a while, she fanned the corners of the pages with her thumb. I watched her carefully, looking for some place in her, an opening, a sentence begun and abandoned, a word. She turned the book over in her lap. She pressed a wrinkle from the cuff of her blouse. We sat there for what seemed like forever without speaking. My head was pounding and getting bigger with each beat of my heart, and my skin was tight across my frame. Fear was the only thing that kept me from reaching out my arms to her, good God Almighty knows I was aching for her. Her eyes were fixed open in a nearly unblinking stare. But by the time Del and my father got home, she was tugging on her top lip with her teeth and hiccuping. When she heard the car door close, she blinked her eyes a few times and sent one single tear down her face. She cleaned her glasses with the hem of her apron, set them back straight on her nose. "You will spend the rest of your life paying for this," she said. Then she dabbed at her mouth and her nose with her handkerchief and handed me a dollar and said, "Go to the store and get me a loaf of bread."

A week later, Del cried quietly in the backseat when Sue Sue and her brother drove me out to the highway. It was only a couple of hours to Plainville, they promised, and their sister Geraldine was expecting me. Del gave me his Syracuse University sweatshirt. When we said our last good-bye, I looked into his eyes, so brown and deep they pulled my heart to the center of the earth. He brushed my cheek with the back of his hand. "Come home soon," he said.

I stayed with Geraldine for about a year. She had five kids of her own and took in ironing. She said she never knew anybody who could get an iron just this side of scorching and never brown a shirt, not till she met me. When I wasn't ironing, I was singing and writing songs, and writing letters to Teddy. These I mailed, but he never answered a one of them. It was like talking off the edge of the world. Somewhere in the middle of the songs and the ironing and out of that emptiness, Jessie was born. Sometimes she seemed to fill that space, and when she didn't, she was always willing to leave me to it.

Jessie looked just like me, and just like Teddy—it was hard to have one without the other because we looked so much alike—and it was sometimes a joy and other times a sorrow. Some days I loved being reminded of him, it was as if the three of us were together. But other days I wanted only to forget him, his memory brought me such pain. In the same way, my songs and my singing went back and forth, rejoicing

Wednesday, wailing Thursday. This finally got on Geraldine's nerves, this and the interest her men friends paid me and my music. It didn't matter how little I cared for them, Geraldine said, because there would come a day when I would take a real shine to just one of them and something ugly would come between us. She asked me to go before that happened.

All these years, and a lot of what I remember is the perpetual leaving. The rest is Jessie and the songs and how inseparable those two have become to me, how I sing to get away from her, to get close to her, to bring her to life, and to quiet her. Sometimes I sing in spite of her, sometimes because of her, and sometimes it's just to remind myself that I sang all my life, and that my music is mine, not hers, or his.

Steve comes back inside just as Jessie wakes up crying. I lift her into my arms and hold her head close to my mouth. "What's the matter, darlin'?" I say softly in her ear.

"I don't feel good," she cries as she nuzzles her head into my shoulder. I hum to her and her crying slowly softens till it's no more than breath.

Steve sits down at the table and picks up his cards. It's my play, but I am fixed on Jessie right now. "You want me to hold her?" Steve asks. I am wishing he would hold me when the phone rings. It sounds like it's his wife. He doesn't say much, except a bunch of yesses and nos, and twice he says, "I said I'd take care of it." Then he hangs up the phone and walks out the door. When he comes back he says, "You have to leave. Which way are you headed?"

"Due north," I say with certainty, my whole body, my

heart and soul pointing the way. "How long a ride is it from here to Syracuse?"

"Not long. Few hours," he says. "You ought to make it tonight, straight shot if you get one ride. Matter of fact, there's a bus due in here in about twenty-five minutes. I know the driver. He'll take you to Binghamton for nothing. I know you're down on your luck, but this just ain't the place for you." He turns on his heel and walks outside to sit on the bumper of a car.

Jessie draws herself from my arms and looks at me like she knows there's something to see. "Come with me to the rest room," I say to her. "We're going to freshen up, and then we're taking the bus to Binghamton."

"What's Binghamton?" she asks.

"It's a town a little ways north of here," I tell her.

"We're going to stay in Binghamton?" she asks.

"No, I don't think so," I say. "We're going to ride the bus there, and then we'll find a way to get to Syracuse."

Jessie rubs her eyes. "Syracuse, you mean home?" she says. "You mean Charlotte and Marcus and Del?"

"Maybe," I say, and I brush her hair back from her face and pull her to me. Years ago, as soon as she was old enough to ask, I told Jessie that we *did* have a home and it was in Syracuse with my mother and father. Not because I believed it, but because she needed to. Now it is my need, and who can promise me we will be welcome there, and safe?

The rain is no more than a drizzle. When the bus pulls up, Steve waves the driver over and the two of them talk alongside

151

the bus. Steve slips the driver some money and gives him a big thump on the back. The driver opens the luggage hold and he and Steve load our things inside. Steve watches me and Jessie cross to the bus. Before we get there, he shakes hands with the driver and walks the other way.

We sit down five seats from the front. There's a handful of passengers, most of them sleeping, the rest looking out the windows. There is no one to talk to, no one wanting to talk to me, just the whine of the engine and the grind of the gears. I wish I could wrap my arms around this firm, well-padded seat, bury myself in it, and cry myself to sleep. We pass through a little town, stop for a couple of lights, and then we're on the highway. The driver throws the bus into gear and I say let it rip, let this tired old bus hurtle us on our way and let this night look for us in Syracuse.

The ride from Pennsylvania into New York State feels like a straight line and I get off the bus knowing we are on our way. The rain has yet to hit Binghamton. It's a slow-moving town. Even in the middle of the afternoon, it looks like it's just waking up. The cop outside the bus station is leaning hard against a brick wall and his face is soft with longing for sleep. I hate to bother him for directions. We cross the street to a coffee shop. I give Jessie a dollar. "Buy some milk and a black coffee. Then see how many doughnuts the change will get you."

Inside the coffee shop, a young guy wearing a funny straw hat is sitting at the counter near the cash register. He talks to

Jessie while the man behind the counter is preparing our order. It must be a cup of hot chocolate the counterman sets down in front of Jessie. She puts her hands on the edge of the counter and sips from the cup. The young guy is still talking to her. She points out the window to me again. He tips his hat. I nod my head.

When our order is ready, Jessie slides from the stool and takes the bag. The young guy pushes her hand aside when she reaches our dollar toward the counterman. Jessie looks out the window at me. I make a sign for her to hurry. He pays and follows Jessie out. At nine years old, my daughter is already like a magnet, drawing men to her. I wonder if she is aware of the tilt of her head, or the way she throws her hip out to one side, her little fingers circling her waist, her shoulder pitched forward at just the right angle. Still, what other skills have I taught her? We have gotten most of what we needed because we were female, because I was female. So she has learned too much of the wrong things, and this afternoon it looks ugly on her.

"Hi, Jeannette, my name is Hugh Bergson," he says, taking his hat off with playful humility. "Jessie tells me you're on your way to Syracuse. I teach at the university. Be glad to give you a ride. That is, if you don't mind stopping to see a movie first." He's tall, probably about six two, and well dressed, everything pressed and cared for. He's got wavy blond hair, with each strand tucked into the right wave. He looks like a college teacher, everything neat and in place, and he's sure of himself, like somebody told him a while back that whatever

153

he wanted would be there when he needed it and he believed them.

"What kind of movie?" I ask him.

"Great movie," he says. "You ever hear of *Some Like It Hot?*"

"No, but I don't see a lot of movies," I say. Somehow, I'd have expected a smoother line.

Jessie says, "Let's go to the movies." She has big dark circles under her eyes. "We don't even have to get popcorn. We've got doughnuts," she says, proud of herself for having thought of it.

"Why don't you go to the movies in Syracuse?" I ask him.

"It's not playing in Syracuse. Listen," he goes on, "my car is around the corner. Wait here and I'll pick you up so we don't have to carry all this stuff." He looks at our bags and boxes. "You sure don't travel light, do you?" he asks. "I hope when you get where you're going you can stay a while."

"So do I," I say. "What's so special about this movie?" I ask him.

"You'll see," he says.

"She gets in half price," I say, pointing to Jessie, "but I don't have the money to pay for either one of us."

"You can be my guests. I'll be right back," he says over his shoulder.

154

We are here on the street waiting for yet another stranger to take us to some strange place. But something has shifted inside me. Life seems filled with possibilities. The cop leaning against the bus-station wall squares his jacket on his shoulders, waves goodnight to the dispatcher in the nearly empty lot, and walks toward his relief, who is headed for the station. I think he too must be going home.

Jessie puts her arm around my waist and rests her head against my hip. "Tired, Jess?" She shakes her head and presses against me a little harder. I like the feeling of our bodies so close.

Hugh pulls up in a white car that looks like an upside-down bathtub. We load everything into the backseat because the trunk is full. The inside is big and sprawling. "What kind of car is this?" I ask him.

"It's a Citroen, made in France," he says.

The car has real leather seats and a shiny wooden dash. Even the little pull-out ashtrays on the doors are trimmed in wood. On the floor in the back are a tennis racket and a pair of shoes, men's dressy shoes, the kind that go with a tuxedo. "Pretty fancy," I say.

"I know," he says, with a smile. "No apologies. I like nice things." He grabs his hat by the brim and places it lightly on my head.

"No thanks," I say and give him back the hat.

"No offense intended," he says. "Would you like to wear it?" he says, offering the hat to Jessie.

"I sure would," she says. It's so big on her it covers nearly her whole face.

"It's too big, Jessie," I say. "Take it off."

"I like it," she says, patting it down over her ears. "I want to wear it."

155

The movie is playing at an old theater downtown. We park right across the street. There's pictures of Marilyn Monroe and Tony Curtis in front. Hugh knows the usher who takes our tickets. "How's the job, Mike?" Hugh asks him as he hands back our stubs.

"It's a good job, if you like the movies," Mike says, "if you like the dark, if you don't have a family to support, or mind the long hours on the weekends."

"I think it's a great job," Jessie says. "I'm going to be a ticket taker when I grow up."

There's a couple of people waiting behind us. Hugh says, "Catch you later." Then he turns to me and says, "I have to have popcorn and I have to sit close." Jessie carries the popcorn and I stop about halfway down the aisle and Hugh says, "Keep going." We sit in the middle of the front row. Seated between the two of us, Jessie looks especially little in Hugh's hat. She thinks this is the most wonderful seat, the most wonderful theater, the best popcorn, the greatest day ever.

After a bunch of coming attractions, Hugh leans over and whispers to me, "I've seen this movie five times. You're going to love it."

I do. So does Jessie. We laugh so hard at the two men dressed up as women we cry. And every time Marilyn Monroe sings, or even just talks, I feel my whole body straining, trying to get near her magic. Jessie keeps saying, "Isn't she beautiful, isn't she beautiful!" and Hugh says, "Absolutely." She is beside herself with pleasure and excitement, jumping out of her chair, kicking her feet up and down, giddy. She has turned the brim of Hugh's hat all the way up. In the darkness, the yellow straw is like a woven halo around her face. When the movie ends, she says, "Let's see it again."

I'm all ready to explain why we can't do that when Hugh says, "Great!"

"You're kidding," I say to him.

"No," he says, "I'm not kidding. Not one bit. They won't charge us to sit through it again. We're only an hour and a half from Syracuse. Why not?"

"I have to go to the toilet," Jessie says. We walk past hundreds of empty seats. The bathroom is all tiled in pink and green. "Isn't it beautiful?" she says. There's a green vinyl chair with skinny black legs in front of a mirror, a little countertop and an ashtray right below the mirror. "You sit down here," Jessie says, "and smoke a cigarette."

She sometimes has very good ideas. I take out the one she got me yesterday morning in Scranton. The room is so quiet I can hear the tobacco burning. The chair is not particularly comfortable, but I like sitting in it, and I like the mirror, the worn-out carpeting, and the dulled tiles.

Jessie stands near me drying her hands with a paper towel. "We ought to take some of these for later." She looks at me quizzically. "How come you're smiling?" she says.

"Who says I'm smiling?" I say.

She turns my face to the mirror with her damp hands that smell like rest-room soap. "See?" she says.

157

"Terrible mistake," I say. "Lost control of the muscles in my face." I turn down the corners of my mouth and furrow my brow. "There. That's better."

"Yes," she says as she takes my arm to lead me back to the movie, "that's much better."

When we get to the front row, Hugh isn't there. I am flooded with fear that he is gone. But his jacket is over the back of his seat and I assure myself he wouldn't have left his jacket if he wasn't coming back. Then I wonder why I care.

Just as they dim the lights, he comes running down the aisle with a big paper bag in his arms and his hair all wet and windblown. "It's pouring out there," he says, throwing himself into his seat, bringing with him a soft cloud that smells unmistakably like hamburgers and french fries. "I love being in the movies when the weather is awful and everybody else is at work," he declares.

Hugh passes out supper by the light of the newsreel. Jessie sets the hat on the empty seat beside me and gives herself over to a chocolate milk shake. Everything is still hot and cold, juicy, tender and crisp, exactly the way it's supposed to be. During the coming attractions Hugh hands me a napkin and says, "You have ketchup all over your face."

I take the napkin from him and stuff it in my pocket. "I know," I say. "I think I look better this way." He wipes a streak of ketchup from my cheek. I take the napkin from my pocket and wipe his finger. I am smiling. Why? It must be the movie. But it's more than that. He doesn't want anything from me, I can feel it. And I'm not looking for anything from him. Because I'm going home, and all I'd be trying to get from him, I'm looking to get from my family. So that's where all my fear is, at home.

The picture starts. I can feel the movie shining off my nose, my cheeks, my eyelashes, like a fine dust. Sitting through the movie the second time makes it mine, every bit of it, the sleeper car, the palm trees, the moon on the water. It makes the theater mine too, the grooves in the arms of the seat, the red upholstery, the tiny tear in the corner of the screen, the sticky floor. I look at Jessie and Hugh. The three of us are sitting in a silvery pool of light.

Jessie sleeps through the second half with her head on Hugh's knee. When the movie ends, I gather up all our papers, napkins and cups and the bag of doughnuts, and Hugh carries Jessie and the hat. In the lobby, he frees a hand to squeeze mine and says, "That was fantastic. I feel great. Thanks for coming with me."

I say, "You're welcome." It's already dark out, the night is blue and black and streaked with wet color. Hugh and I trade freight and I hug Jessie closer to me as he unlocks the door. "You're being very kind to us," I say to him. "Why?"

He looks at me with eyes which are suddenly heavy lidded and watery. "Because you need it and I have it." He pauses. "Because it's a kindness with a beginning and an end." The sky has cleared and there is a hurry and a secret to the heavy swishing sound of moving cars on the wet streets. Hugh is still speaking, something about life and chance meetings, saying good-bye, saying hello. Jessie's chest is rising and falling against mine in the perfect breathing of her sleep. My bottom lip is trembling and I am awash in feelings I cannot describe.

The city seems to end all at once and we are traveling north on 11, each of us riding in our own silence. In the blindness of the night I try to separate my memories of the past—my life and Jessie's, 1951 to 1960—from my hopes and fears of the future. I am afraid of every possibility equally. The thought that my parents might be happy to see me, that my mother might open her heart to me in a way she wouldn't a lifetime ago, that my brother might teach Jessie to ride a bike, that my father might pour hot butterscotch syrup on a bowl of vanilla ice cream and serve it to me on a tray, such thoughts make me quake as bad as the visions of pointing fingers, pursed lips, and turned backs.

The wind is picking up, and it's raining again. Hugh's car may be nice, but it's only got one headlight and no first gear. His face is lit dimly by the lights from the dash. He's handsome in a fussy kind of way. I am suddenly aware of the dampness in the car, of my clothes heavy with three days of sweat. I remember noticing that I looked like a bum when I sat in front of the mirror at the movies, but I didn't pay it much mind. Now it's all I can think of. I'm not accustomed to riding alongside a man who by the very looks of him is out of my league. In fact, most of the men who've driven me across town or across country, who've fed me or had me feed them have opened their car doors and their front doors to me, and to Jessie, because I was exactly in their league, because

I put myself in their league, and any time I thought I was better than them, there was always this: If I was so damned special, what the hell was I doing with them? And if I was too proud to ask myself the question, they surely weren't.

Hugh asks me to light him a cigarette. We pass a sign north of Cortland that says SYRACUSE 25 MILES. Jessie is fidgeting with the radio dials, pulling in nothing but static until she hits a station playing a Bo Diddley tune. Hugh says, "Leave that." Jessie recognizes the song. She tells him about the D.C. club where we heard Bo Diddley last year with Lydia, a toothless evangelist preacher lady. "You like Bo Diddley?" he asks her.

"Not as much as Jeannette," she says, and she smiles her biggest smile at me when she adds, "and she sings just like him."

Hugh looks at me through his bushy blond eyebrows and says, "I never would have figured you to be the Bo Diddley type."

"I'm not any type," I say, "but I like his songs and I like the way he sings them. Still, even if I was to try to sound exactly like him, I couldn't because our voices are so different."

"Well, just for starters," Hugh says, "you're a girl and he's a guy."

"Well, anybody could figure that out," Jessie says, saving me the trouble. "But that's not the only difference between them," she adds.

"What is it then?" Hugh says.

Jessie shrugs her shoulders and grins.

"Do you think you can get some work singing in Syracuse?" he asks.

"I haven't thought that far ahead," I say.

"Well, you ought to," he tells me, "and you ought to start thinking about it now, because we're only a couple of miles away from a joint that has live music every night of the week. It just so happens I know the manager."

"Yes, so what?" I ask.

"So what?" he asks. "So let's stop in and have a beer, see if this guy is around. What do you say, Jessie?"

"What time is it?" I ask.

"What difference does it make what time it is? Is somebody waiting up for you? Do you have an appointment in the morning?"

"What's it to you?"

"It's nothing to me. I'm just the kind of person who likes to seize an opportunity, and I thought you might be the same kind of person."

"It's not always easy to tell an opportunity from a waste of time," I say.

"I guess that's the chance you have to take. And excuse me," he goes on, "but judging from the shape the two of you are in, I wouldn't have thought your time was so spare." He puts his right blinker on and Jessie asks where we're going. Hugh doesn't answer her. We pull into a parking lot with a half dozen cars alongside a frame building. A blinking Genesee sign lights up the front window. "Anyway, if you don't want to come in, you can wait in the car," Hugh says. "I'd like to get myself something to drink, but I won't be long."

I'm reluctant to follow him because I hate how damned sure of himself he is. But there's a rare and precious pleasure in being guided. Jessie looks at me as she climbs out of the car and bounds after Hugh.

The bar is called Troop's and the best thing about it is that it's dry inside, except for a leak right by the door. Hugh motions for me to join him and Jessie at the bar, where he is talking with a man who looks about as ugly as anybody I've seen in a while, even from across the room. After Hugh introduces us, he takes Jessie over to the jukebox.

The guy's name is Lloyd Potter. "Not much of a crowd here tonight," he says to me in an oily voice. Close up, he looks even uglier, skinny, thinning yellow hair plastered down to his head, bad skin, and he's wearing a nasty looking western shirt, green and yellow flowers on a black background. "Hugh tells me you're a singer."

"Musician," I say, "I'm a musician, I sing and I write music too."

"Is that so?" he says. "Isn't that something, sings and writes music too." He gives me a squinty smile that shows his bad teeth, little teeth to start with, and discolored from cigarettes. "You a soloist?" he asks.

"Yes, I am," I say.

"Cigarette?" he asks and he offers me a crumpled package of Winstons and a light. "I usually like to book groups," he says with his own cigarette hanging out of the corner of his mouth and the smoke rising up into his eyes. "People around

163

here like a group. We have amateur nights on Mondays. Why don't you come around some Monday night?" He gives me another wide and squinty smile, and turns to walk away.

It occurs to me that Hugh has never met this guy before. Well, I can keep up with him. "In the first place," I say, talking to Potter through my own cigarette now and taking a kind of twisted pleasure in the smoke that is burning my eyes, "I'm not an amateur. In the second place I've got my guitar in the car, so if you're interested in what I sound like, you can find out real fast."

"Well," he says as he turns toward the bar and picks up the telephone, "we're having trouble with our wiring and I don't expect you have an amp with you anyway . . ."

"I play acoustic, and I don't need a mike," I say on my way to the door. Jessie and Hugh are off in a corner dancing to "Rave On." The room feels warm and cozy with a handful of people at a couple of tables.

Outside, the rain is like little pellets flung from a low sky, stinging my face and neck. I dig my guitar out from under the bags and bundles and tear inside. Potter has his back to me and the phone to his ear. I set my guitar on the bar and ask the bartender for a glass of water. I take my battered blond Martin out of the case and tune the strings in the half-assed way you do when there's music playing.

I start out with the opening chords to "Maybelline," soft and sweet like a ballad. My ribs rattle. Lord, it feels fine. Potter hangs up the phone and dials another number. The new Del Shannon hit is just finishing. Hugh unplugs the

jukebox. He and Jessie sit down at a table near the other end
of the bar. I start to pick up a little bit. I fire the verses like
hot peppers, and stretch out that name, "Oh, Maybelli-i-i-ne,
why can't you be tru-u-u-e," teasing my way through the
song, singing to every man I ever needed and knew I could
get, pushing through with the music and ignoring the feeling
of Hugh's eyes on me. Potter hangs up the telephone and
turns about a quarter of the way around, still looking like he's
not listening. I go right into a Bo Diddley song. "Don't you
know the Lord above, / Created you just for me to love"—the
verses are a place to play and flirt, but the refrain is where I
live—"Dearest darling, oh, oh, oh," wrapping every sound
around myself. My eyes are shut tight but I'm seeing red,
drawing each breath from the soles of my tingling feet, feeling
that thing rise up in me that comes from the spirit and drives
the body. I finish with "Long Gone Lover." I'm in a trance.

When I open my eyes Potter is lighting another cigarette.
"That was good, Jeannette." I take the cigarette and light he
offers me. "We might be able to use you, maybe on a Wednesday night. We get a pretty good crowd on Wednesdays." He
flicks his cigarette ash onto the floor. "Say the Wednesday
after next. That'll give us time to get out some notices, plug
you on the radio. See if we can't get some people out to hear
you."

"Wednesday after next sounds fine," I say. The room feels
very big now, and Jessie and Hugh look far away. Somebody
gets up from one of the tables and plugs the jukebox back in.
A guy from the same table walks over to where I'm standing.

He says his name and thanks me for singing. He says everybody at his table thought I was terrific. I tell him I'm glad they liked it. He tells Potter he ought to hire me. Potter looks at him like he's a big black fly. I don't think it shows on the outside, but inside I feel like I'm coming apart.

"Plan to be here around eight-thirty," Potter says, "play a few sets, take a couple of breaks, stay till around one." Jessie and Hugh are on their way across the room, one of them smiling bigger than the other, though I can't say which. "By the way," Potter says, "you get ten bucks plus your meal for the night." I know they pay more than ten dollars. I can tell he doesn't like me personally but he knows I'm too good to pass up. So I'm going to show up here in a couple of weeks just like I said. If I'm still around.

Jessie reaches for my neck and pulls me down so I can kiss her. She whispers in my ear that I'm wonderful, that I'm the best singer in the world. Hugh is shooting me smiles and a thumbs-up while he is saying good-bye to Potter. He picks up my guitar and says to me in a grand voice, "May I see you to your car, madam?"

He holds the door for me and Jessie. As soon as we are in the car, he says, "I'd tell you how great you were, but I think you already know." He puts his arm around my shoulder, and even in the dark I can feel he is looking deep into my eyes. "I don't think he was quite expecting anything like you," he says. Then he makes a cute little chuckle and adds, "Matter of fact, neither was I." He stretches his arm out so that it rests easy on the back of the seat. Jessie reaches up to plant another kiss on my cheek, and then she kisses Hugh's hand. I bless her warmth toward him, though I fear it too. I know how she must long for a father, for the promise of protection. But I suspect my fear has as much to do with what I know of myself as it has to do with what I sense about Jessie. I have longings of my own.

The rain is really coming down now. The wipers are down to metal. Hugh drives slow, looking for a place on the windshield where he can see the road. Jessie is sleeping again, limp and heavy on the seat between us. I'm afraid to ask what time it is. If we get into town too late, we can't go to my mother's house, not after nine. And if it's after nine, I don't know where we'll go. I've spent the night in more than one bus station, but never in Syracuse.

Hugh gets off the highway to stop for some gas right outside the city. The clock over the garage says nine forty-five. "It's late," I say.

"Late for what?" he says as he pulls back onto the road.

"Late for me to walk in on my mother and father after an unexplained absence of nearly ten years," I say. Hugh whistles. "What time do you think I could be on Euclid Avenue?"

"Maybe another twenty minutes," he says. "Do you want to give them a call?"

"Give them a call?" I say. "I don't know. What would I say?"

Hugh looks at me and says, "You're asking *me*?"

"No, I don't think I want to call them," I answer.

As we drive up North Adams Street, I remember myself

standing here, my inexperienced thumb pointing the way for the first time. Even in this downpour, I know where we are. Most everything is familiar, except for what's strange, a new building put up, an old one torn down, the TV repair shop, which once had a beautiful pink neon Motorola sign in the window, boarded up, a life remembered and forgotten pulling me both backward and forward.

Things are much the same on our block. By the glow of the street lamps, I can make out this sign of spring, the trees lightly misted with the softness that comes before budding leaves. There is still one house with Christmas lights in the window. The Wilmores have finished their garage and built a carport for their prized '36 Chevrolet. A shiny new 1960 Buick is parked in our driveway. It hits me that it may not be our driveway anymore, we may not live here now. It may be some other family's. Of all the things I have imagined about coming home, this is the most bewildering. But equally bewildering is the sight of my brother, Del, a twenty-four-year-old man now, handsome, as near as I can tell, in a red windbreaker, dragging the garbage can from the garage out to the street. He looks up at us, at the car, and then lowers his head again to duck the rain.

"Who's that?" Hugh asks.

"My brother," I say.

"Aren't you going to say hello?"

"Not tonight," I say. "It's too late."

"Too late?" he echoes. "That's a lot of bullshit. Ten years is so late there's no such thing as late."

Hugh's judgment sounds like something I've heard before. We sit in the car without saying a word for a couple of minutes. "I'd like to wait till morning," I say. "I don't know exactly why, I'd just like to wait until tomorrow."

"Wait where?" Hugh says.

"Bus station," I say. "Just drop us off at the bus station."

"Oh, no," he says, "no you don't. I drop you off at the bus station, and you take the first bus out of here headed nowhere, and any place you go from here is nowhere. Listen, I don't know where you've been or what's been moving you from one place to another, but from the looks of things, it's about time to stop. You don't want to see your family until the morning, okay. You and Jessie come and spend the night with me. In the morning, after you shower and put on some clean clothes, I'll drive you over here."

I wish to hell this cost him something, because I would be happy to sit in this car on this dark night in the tireless rain, cradling my little girl beside this Hugh forever.

My head feels heavy and light at the same time. There's a fog-covered half moon just kissing the tops of the elm trees. Del lowers the garage door, shuts off the light, and closes the front door behind him.

169

He doesn't come on real strong. He just lets me know that if I don't want to sleep alone, if I just want the company, I'm welcome to sleep with him. Otherwise, I can sleep alongside Jessie on the big couch in the living room, and there are blankets enough for all of us. While I am taking a shower, I can hear the TV in his bedroom. It sounds like *The Jack Parr Show*. I loosen my braid and swish the shampoo through my hair under the hot water. The suds turn a sooty brown, days of automobile exhaust, dirty seat covers, and cigarette smoke swirling in the drain. From among the neatly lined-up contents of the medicine cabinet, I find a bottle of lotion. My legs and arms are strangely unfamiliar to my hand as I smooth puddles of white cream on my skin. I put on a robe hanging on the back of the bathroom door and sit down on the floor to towel-dry my hair. I smoke a cigarette and trace the black-and-white tiles of the floor with my finger. Then I smoke another cigarette.

I hear the TV go off in Hugh's room. His light is out and the door is open when I walk down the hall toward the living room. The walls of this passage are lined with framed photographs of movie stars and pictures of scenes from movies. I wonder where the pictures of his parents, his grandparents, his girlfriend are. In the living room the furniture is very modern and elegant. The walls are mostly bare, except for a large, sparkling mirror above the sofa and a painting on fabric—it looks like it's from Japan or China—near the dining-room table. Hugh's home is strangely bare but very beautiful.

There's a stack of blankets and pillows piled on the coffee table. Jessie has not moved from the end of the sofa where I laid her down when we first came in. I take off her shoes and jacket and cover her with a quilt.

With the lamp turned off and the room dark, a big slab of

the floor near the window is bright with a square of light cast by a street lamp and crossed with shadows from a tree. When the wind blows, the shadows dance in the square. With a blanket underneath me to save my back from the cold of the floor, and another on top of me, I lie down in the square to let the light and shadows play on my face. Sometimes the wind is so strong the shadows flicker violently and the room seems to rock. But I am still. I am lying six inches above the floor, nearly weightless, floating. Jessie is floating too, just above the sofa. Then I am standing outside, my feet kneading the dark soil and mulch of wet leaves left by winter and the wind, my elbows set on the window ledge, watching the floating woman and the floating little girl inside the room.

The sound of a police siren a few blocks away wakes me. It's still dark outside but the wind has died down and the rain has ended. I go to the kitchen for a glass of water and then walk back toward the couch. A light in the bathroom draws me down the hall to the door to Hugh's bedroom. When he comes out of the bathroom he smiles at me, takes my hand, and leads me to his bed. I feel like I haven't felt in too long, my whole self alive with exhaustion and wanting, not one bit of me holding back or uncertain.

The morning comes shy but with open eyes. In the growing light I see Hugh's room, the bed, his desk, a big overstuffed chair piled high with books, then Jessie at the door. Hugh sees her first. "Come on in, Jess," he says.

She's standing just inside the room in the clothes she's been wearing for three days. She looks tired and cross. "No,

Hugh," I say to him. "Jessie, I'll be out in a little while. Go back to sleep." As she walks back down the hall I hear and feel her little heels driving into the floor. I turn on my stomach and dig my fingers into the pillow. Hugh cracks the knuckles of his fingers one at a time. Then he pulls the sheet over my shoulders and rests his hand on the back of my neck. It's a nice gesture but it's not enough.

It's just after seven. Jessie is sleeping again, her arms clutching a small pillow, her face turned into the corner of the couch. In the kitchen I roll myself a couple of cigarettes and make a cup of tea. My mother must be just getting up. My father's probably been up for a while, him and Del sitting at the kitchen table talking about I don't know what. I'll wait till around ten. I'll have Hugh drop us off at the corner. There won't be anybody home then but my mother. She'll be listening to the radio and washing the dishes, or maybe ironing. I'll knock on the door first, but then I'll just let myself in. She won't even hear us. Jessie will be looking around at everything, the furniture, the polished floors, the curtains. I'll call out to my mother so we won't frighten her; I'll say, "Mrs. Keller."

Maybe it would be better if I call from the porch, just open the door enough so she can hear me say her name. I'll let Jessie wait in the car or stand on the sidewalk for a minute till I tell her to come inside. But it might be that my mother has a job herself now. Maybe there won't be anybody home, or maybe just Del. He'll recognize the car from last night if he's bringing in the garbage can or looking out the window when we drive up. He'll open the door and watch us walk up the sidewalk to the porch. He'll come and stand outside with us, offer me a cigarette. He'll ask me who's in the car, do we want to come in, do I want a cup of coffee, do I still play the guitar, what's the little girl's name. He'll sit with us for a while, nobody will say anything much. Then he'll say he has to leave for work. We'll be awkward with each other, I know. It's going to take some time.

Hugh comes into the kitchen and pours himself a glass of orange juice. "It's kind of dark in here. Why don't you put on a light?" he says.

"I guess it is dark," I say. "I hadn't really noticed."

"Good," he says, "because it looks like it might not clear up today at all. Not much of a day for a homecoming. Pretty dreary for the fourth of April."

"Is that today's date?" I say.

"That it is," he says.

"It's my mother's birthday," I say.

"You could put a ribbon in your hair and tell her you're a surprise birthday present," he says, smiling at me playfully and smoothing my brow with the back of his hand. "What time do you want me to take you over there?"

"About ten," I say. "If that's okay with you."

"Could we make it nine-thirty?" he says. "I have a class to teach at ten, and I have to park the car."

"Nine-thirty is fine," I say. I light another cigarette and inhale deeply. Hugh puts a little piece of paper in my hand

and says, "Here's my address and phone number. I'll be home around four. Call me, and I'll bring your things over to you whenever you like." My heart is beating so fast I can't talk, can't ask all the questions, about him and this morning, and the other questions, about me and Jessie, because for just a moment I think he understands things I can't make sense of and right now I'd give the world for some sense. But then I look at him. There is no disturbance on his face, no regret in the way he holds his shoulders or hesitation in the way he drinks his coffee. I suspect that there is something missing in him, something that dried up in the middle of a movie and left in its absence a home filled with pictures of strangers. He smiles at me as he walks from the kitchen, and I scold myself for such ungrateful thoughts.

I stir a big spoonful of Hershey's into a glass of milk and bring it to Jessie. She's lying on her back now with her mouth wide open. "Jess, it's time to get up," I say and shake her a little. She opens her eyes and looks at me. Then she closes them again and her face is set like a plaster mask. "I got some chocolate milk here for you," I say. She sits up and takes the glass like she is doing me a favor. "Then you and me are going to jump into the shower together and put on something nice and go over to see your grandparents."

"Charlotte and Marcus? And Del?" she asks through a long gulp, breathless and excited in spite of herself. I wonder at her ability to believe and trust me still. I smile at her and nod my head yes, and then I put my arms around her. Lord, she is so small. I must forget how little she is sometimes, or it wouldn't feel like such a surprise to me now. "We better hurry," she says, breaking free of my embrace.

She finds her way to the bathroom and has her clothes off by the time I catch up with her. She's dried off and sprinkling her slinky skinny body with talcum powder from a shelf above the john as I step out of the shower. She runs a comb through her hair and says to me on her way out the door, "I'm going to pick out my clothes." When I join her in the living room a few minutes later, she is proudly modeling an all-orange outfit for Hugh, orange-and-green checkered pants, an orange sweater, and orange socks.

"Do you think this is a good outfit to sing 'Happy Birthday' in?" I ask her.

"Whose birthday?" she asks.

"Your grandmother's," I say.

"Yes," she says. "Get dressed," she adds. "I'm ready to go." She checks the cuffs of her pants and pats her still-damp hair into place over and over. I remember her face at Hugh's bedroom door this morning. Now she is all business.

Hugh picks up a stack of books from a chair and says he'll wait for us in the car. Jessie looks nervous now, picking fretfully at a little hole in the elbow of her sweater while she hums "Happy Birthday" under her breath, trying out different keys and tempos. I pull on the first dress I've worn in months and dig a pair of flats out of one of our bags. I'm nervous and sweating so bad I've got a chill.

Hugh and Jessie talk the whole ten minutes to our house. When he stops to let us out across the street from 37 Euclid

Avenue, Jessie says, "Look, is that Marcus leaving?" She points to the powder-blue Skylark pulling out of the driveway. Even at a distance of twenty feet, my father seems like he's within arm's reach, those familiar dark glasses perched on the end of his nose, his chin a good hour ahead of the rest of him. He's alone and doesn't even look our way.

"Well," Jessie says, "I hope Charlotte is still home." She jumps from the car and runs up the walk to the porch. I get out of the car and close the door behind me. Standing on this street, I am sealed off from the world, alone and afraid. I swallow a cry and hold my hand back from reaching out to Hugh as he drives away. The kiss he blows to me from the corner is less than I want, but it keeps me standing while Jessie rings the bell.

My mother opens the door. She is wearing a crisply pressed housedress, a beautiful floral print of pale pink and sky blue, and a navy sweater over her shoulders. She's taken to dyeing her hair and somehow it makes her look older instead of younger, but it draws her features in sharper relief, makes her eyes especially dark behind her glasses.

Just as she opens her mouth to speak to the little girl at her door, Jessie starts to sing. She sings "Happy Birthday" through and ends it with "dear Charlotte." My mother looks pleased but puzzled. She looks up from Jessie to me, just as Jessie is beginning the song again. Her face settles into a stare that shows no feeling all the while Jessie is singing. This time when Jessie comes to the end she adds, "dear Grandma." My mother's lips part like she is going to smile, but she seems to think better of it and closes her mouth again. Then she takes Jessie's hand and walks her to the front of the porch. She brushes off a place for herself and a place for Jessie on the top step, and when they are both sitting down, my mother says, "Would you please sing that to me once more, and after that, if you have any other songs you know, I'd like very much to hear them."

Jessie says, "Okay, but Jeannette sings better than me."

"I know," my mother says, "but I'm not ready to hear her just yet."

Jessie begins "Happy Birthday" again. After that she sings "Give Me a Little Kiss." Sometimes my mother watches her, sometimes she just looks down at her own feet or plays with the buttons of her sweater or pushes her glasses up on her nose. At first I feel small and invisible, then I feel gigantic, then I feel invisible again. After Jessie finishes "Rock Around the Clock" she says, "Can we go inside? I'm cold."

"Yes, we can," my mother says, as she stands up and takes Jessie's hand.

Jessie looks out to where I'm standing. "What about Jeannette?" she asks.

"She'll be in in a little while," my mother says. She opens the door and Jessie goes inside. My mother stands for a minute. I can see her thinking right through her back. Then she takes her sweater off and lays it on the porch railing. When the door is closed and they are gone from sight, I go up the porch steps and put the sweater around my shoulders. It's still warm from my mother and smells like her perfume. I try

177

to think of a song to sing, but I can't remember a single tune. My mother's sweater is tight around my shoulders. I think I may be taller than her. I'm glad when Mr. Wilmore comes out of his house next door and brushes some leaves off his Chevy. He looks at me a couple of times. On his way back into the house he waves at me and I wave back. When the door closes behind him, I say, "Hello, Mr. Wilmore. How are you doing this morning, Mr. Wilmore?" Then I answer myself, "I'm fine, Jeannette. Thank you for asking. We're glad to see you back." I'd laugh at myself for going on this way except that it feels so good.

There's a rap on the window. It gives me a start and sets my heart pounding, or maybe it's been pounding all along. Jessie is standing by my father's lounge chair and pointing to the front door, which my mother opens very quietly—if I wasn't watching, I might not have noticed. As it is I notice everything, the sound of her low-heeled shoes on the bare floor as she walks toward the kitchen, the white voile curtain on the door rippling in the wind, the turned-up edge on the oval rag rug in the hall, the sound of the door as I close it behind me.

Jessie is sitting in my father's lounger, rocking back and forth. "Grandma says I can sleep in your old room," she says, and then she adds, "all by myself."

"Is that so?" I say, amazed that my voice is steady. "And where does Grandma say I can sleep?"

"She didn't say," Jessie answers.

My mother calls from the kitchen, "Jessie, come pick out some jam for your toast."

"Are you having breakfast?" I ask Jessie.

"Yes, I am. Scrambled eggs and toasted white bread. I can have one piece of toast now while I'm waiting. And I'm having tea. With milk and sugar." Is there something vindictive about the way she prances across the room? Is there meanness in her bounce or just pleasure and self-confidence? My young daughter marches into the kitchen with an air of possession unlike anything I have ever seen from her, the way she would have marched into Hugh's bedroom this morning if I'd let her.

I follow her into the kitchen. My mother is filling the sugar bowl from the canister Del and I gave her for Christmas the last year we lived in Tennessee. She says to Jessie, "Would you like to take a walk with me to the store? I have no milk for your tea. We'll buy something for lunch, too. You can show me what you like."

Jessie catches herself as she is about to ask me if she can go. Instead she answers her grandmother, "Yes, I'll go with you to the store. I like banana-and-mayonnaise sandwiches for lunch. Can we buy some bananas?"

My mother looks at me as she asks Jessie, "Where did you learn to eat such a thing?"

"From Juan," Jessie answers. "We lived with him in . . ."

"Never mind," my mother interrupts. Then she thinks again and says, "Forgive me, Jessie. I'm sorry I didn't let you finish. Where was that you were living?"

"In Ohio. Juan had a pickup truck and he took us to the drive-in every week. At Halloween, he made paper cutouts of skeletons and taped them up on all the windows and lit candles everywhere. He called me 'Jessita.' "

My mother looks at Jessie like she is trying to read in her face all the other stories. She runs her fingers across her chin and says, "That's very nice. How about a banana for dessert and ham and cheese for your sandwich?"

"Ham and cheese and mayonnaise?" Jessie asks.

"Yes," my mother says. I feel like they are planning meals for the next year, and I am a ghost with no appetite. My mother takes a few dollars from her wallet and they leave by the back door. As my mother closes the door behind her, she looks at me through the window curtained with taut gathers of lace. I cannot read her.

The store is two blocks away. They will walk slowly so that my mother can pay close attention to Jessie. Jessie will talk all the way. She will tell my mother more about Juan and Ohio, and about Detroit and Albuquerque. Maybe she will tell her about Hugh and the movie. Let her tell everything, or as much as she knows. I am finished with hiding.

Alone in the house, I walk through the rooms of the first floor, marking to myself the changes. On the mantel in the living room is a photograph of my mother and father seated before a large frosted cake with the number 25 glittering on top. In the dining room, the chairs have been reupholstered in a horrible striped material, peach and green, my mother's favorite colors. By the stairs to the second floor is a large box marked SALVATION ARMY. It's filled with old clothes, some of which I recognize—a flannel shirt that once belonged to Preston, which Teddy and I wore when Preston tired of it, a pair of pajamas that were a Christmas gift from me to Del the last winter I was home. Next to the box, leaning against the banister, is a pair of crutches. Someone in my family broke a leg or an ankle while I was gone. The rubber tips are worn and split, well used. The injury took a long time to heal. I try them, but they are too tall for me. It was Del or my father who hobbled around for—how long—a winter? a year? Without me.

"Jeannette?" How can Del have come halfway down the stairs without my hearing him? He stops, comes no closer. He lowers himself slowly till he is sitting on the edge of a step, his arms wrapped tightly around his knees. His eyes are bright and his hair is still wet from his shower. "I thought I heard voices," he says.

"It was Mom and Jessie. Jessie is my daughter. She's nine. I've told her all about you. She wants you to teach her to curl her tongue. I think she has the right kind of tongue. I can't teach her because I don't have the right kind of tongue." I wish he would interrupt me because I don't think I can stop talking. "She can roll a perfect cigarette, too. She used to do them real sloppy, too much spit, but she's been at it for . . ."

"Where've you been?" he asks.

"What?"

His eyes are cutting holes in my head. "Where the hell have you been?"

I know he doesn't really want me to answer this question, but I find myself reciting anyway. "All over. Fort Wayne, Indiana, New Mexico, Michigan. I spent a while in Ohio, we lived in Cleveland and Columbus."

"Ten years," he says, and now it feels more like I'm being cast out into the wilderness than come home from it. He bites at the nail of one of his fingers, looks at me, looks away, presses his fist against his mouth. "You've been gone ten years. What the hell have you been doing?" He rises from the step and is at my side and shaking me by the shoulders. "Ten years, and never a word. Why? How could you do that?" His face is red, his eyes too. He digs his fingers deeper into me. His hands are huge, his fingers strong. I can't tell whether he is pressing me into the floor or holding me up. Then he pushes me away, only an arm's distance, and with the next breath draws me to him. In his embrace I begin to tremble. It starts around my ankles, my feet rattle in my shoes. It goes up my legs and sets my skirt to rustling, past my hips so I feel like I'm standing on stilts, and makes my head wobble on my neck. I can't say a word, but Del is sobbing, loud in my ear, "Oh, my God, Jeannette, you're home." Please, dear Lord, let me die right now.

The telephone rings. Del drops one arm from around me to wipe his nose with the back of his hand. Then he brushes my cheek with the other hand. "I better get that," he says. He crosses to the telephone in the living room and clears his throat as he raises the receiver to his mouth. "Hello . . . I know, I overslept. I'm on my way . . . I'll be there in just a while." He hangs up the phone.

"You late for work?"

"Yes. We opened a hardware store. Bought out Al Freeman's stock when he closed. Dad's on his way to Utica to look at some brass findings he thinks he can sell. I got to hold things down." He smiles bashfully with pride. Then he looks at me again. "Is this you?" He scans my body as though he's checking to see if all my parts are still attached. "How are you?"

"I'm okay. A little shook, I guess."

"You already talked to Mom?"

"Not really. I mean, she isn't talking to me yet. She's half pretending I'm not here, like Jessie arrived by magic."

"We'll close early. Dad and me, we'll come home early. Around three. He ought to be back by then." His face freezes with surprise and then melts into a smile. "Wait till I tell Dad. Jesus, Jeannette, he's going to be so excited. Maybe I should try to reach him in Utica."

"Could you hold off, Del? Just give me the morning here. Three o'clock sounds fine. Is it unfair of me to ask? Please, say something."

"No, I guess it's all right. Probably work out perfectly." He looks at his wristwatch. "If I go now, I can grab a ride with Mrs. Wilmore."

I follow him to the kitchen. He splashes some cold water on his face and runs a comb through his hair. "Where'd Mom go?"

"She and Jessie went to the store."

"Look at this. *Me,* I'm talking to *you.* 'Where'd Mom go?' "
He shakes his head in disbelief. His eyes are even darker than
they were ten years ago, and his lashes thick and black as
smoke. If this is the only moment of pleasure I get from
coming home, it was worth it. "Are you going to be here
later?"

"Yes." He wants more. "Absolutely."

"Are you going to be okay?"

"I'm fine. I'll be fine."

"I'm going to go, then. Walk me to the door." He puts his
arm around my shoulder. On the front porch, he takes my
hand and presses it to his cheek. "See you later."

"See you later."

The front door swings open with an easy tug. I know it's
silly, but I so like the way it yields to my hand. My mother's
breakfast plates clatter on the table as I set three places. I fold
three napkins into long triangles, no, rectangles, no, anchor
them under each dish and hang them from the edge of the
table like bibs. The kitchen feels stuffy. The window over the
sink sticks at first, then gives to the slam of the heel of my
hand. The leaves of my mother's purple passion vibrate in the
breeze.

My mother and Jessie arrive in the backyard and stand on
the porch, discussing the height of the clothesline. Jessie says
she can reach it. My mother says Del can lower the line a few
inches and still keep the sheets from the ground. Jessie insists

the height is perfect for her. My mother says they can try it together this afternoon, maybe Jessie is right.

The screen door needs oiling. Jessie sets a bag on the counter and takes a place at the table.

"Did you enjoy your walk?" I ask her.

"I saw everything," she says.

"What did you see?"

"Houses, cars, the school, the church, the swimming pool in somebody's backyard, a cat on a leash, an old lady hollering at the postman, a little girl hanging upside down from a tree. I'm hungry."

My mother lights a flame under the kettle and puts two slices of bread in the toaster. "Ask your mother if she would like some tea," she says to Jessie.

I hang my mother's sweater over the back of a chair.

"Yes, I would like a cup of tea."

"Ask your mother," my mother continues, "if she would like to wash before breakfast. I believe Del is done in the bathroom."

"Del left for work. We saw each other."

"You saw Del?" Jessie asks excitedly. "Did you tell him about me? Did you tell him I'm here?"

"Yes, of course I told him you're here. He's coming home at three with your grandfather. They can't wait to meet you."

185

"Oh," Jessie says with a worried look, "Grandma and me are going shopping for some new clothes at two." She turns to my mother. "Can we be home by three, Grandma?"

"We certainly can," my mother answers as she butters the toast and places it before Jessie. "Or we can go shopping another time. Tomorrow. Or the next day." She takes a glass down from the cupboard and hands it to Jessie. "Can you pour yourself a glass of milk? And ask your mother if she would like some juice."

"Ask your grandmother," I instruct Jessie, "when she is going to talk to me."

The kettle is whistling. My mother turns the flame down and says to Jessie, "Tell her not till I am good and ready."

"When will that be?" I ask and I look at her, willing her to answer me.

"It's hard to say," she says, suddenly looking me square in my face. I am startled: We are standing so close. Her words, heavy and ancient, wrap me in shock. "It took you quite a while, didn't it? I don't think I move quite that slow, but surely you don't imagine you can waltz back into this house without accounting for all the harm you've done and all the pain you've caused?"

How many times have I dreamed of this moment, but never did I imagine myself so righteous, knowing now what I have never let myself know before. "I didn't do it alone. I did the leaving, but you left me to go, never took one step toward finding me, and you could have with less trouble than it probably took to forget me. A year and a half in Plainville, Geraldine's a few hours away, and you never even called. You went on without me. I know you're angry, but it seems to me at least half of it's guilt turned sour." I hold tightly to the top of Jessie's chair to keep my hands, my arms, from flying off my shoulders. "Mother, I was only a child."

In a gesture I have never seen before, my mother tucks her hands under her arms and presses her elbows against her waist. "How must you have lived all these years to speak of my guilt so shamelessly? Dear God, Jennie, forget you? Not for one day. How do you forget a wound that never heals?"

Standing still, in one place, is the hardest thing I have ever done. I want to grab Jessie's hand, run back to Hugh's apartment house, climb in a window, fly to the bathroom, close the door behind me, sit on the floor, and smoke all the cigarettes in the world.

Jessie picks up a piece of toast and takes a bite. Her little shoulders heave in silent sobs as she crams more of the toast into her mouth. My mother looks from me to Jessie, back and forth. Jessie's eyes are filling up with tears and her head begins to shake. I want to touch her, to stroke her forehead and kiss the back of her neck, but my whole body seems fixed and frozen. My mother, too, seems unable to move.

I am frightened by the first thing I hear, Jessie coughing, crying and sputtering, choking on her toast. Yet, for a moment, I hesitate, fascinated by the sound, as though it isn't connected to her, or to anyone, just a sound. Then I'm alert again, kneeling at her side, patting her back firmly. "Put your arms up, Jessie," I tell her, and raise my own arms to encourage her. Her thin little arms in her orange sweater rise slowly. She is still crying, but the choking has stopped. Her nose is running and her mouth and cheeks are covered with toast crumbs. I put my arms around her shoulders and draw her to me, but her arms are still in the air. From behind, I feel my mother's shadow as she guides Jessie's arms around my neck. Then I hear her say, "There, there, it's okay, sweetheart, it's okay, darling." I imagine she is talking to me. Then I feel the warmth of her body, her arms around me, her fingers stretching to include Jessie in her embrace.

You can't stay like that, all wrapped up in each other, but for so long. My mother moves first, stands up and straightens the belt and the collar on her dress. Then Jessie pushes me away gently and reaches for a napkin to wipe her face and nose. "I have to use the toilet," she says.

"The bathroom," my mother corrects her sweetly, "is at the top of the stairs."

Jessie touches everything within reach of her fingers on her way out of the kitchen. Her sticky, tearstained hands jump in pretty arches from chair to rotisserie to light switch. Is she counting or claiming?

My mother washes her hands at the kitchen sink and dries them carefully, slowly, as though she had nothing to do for the rest of her life. The room is still ringing with our words. If I take a step, I will walk into one of them, or something else out of place, a day from among all the years I've been gone, a day from among all the years I was here. I feel suddenly exhausted. The room is shrinking, and then the walls are speeding away from each other. I am dizzy and heavy-headed at the same time, and I cannot catch my breath. I let myself out the back door.

Here, among the newly green branches of the lilac bushes, there is air. My head clears as the wind drives high, obedient clouds across the sky. It seems as if a clear glass dome has been dropped over the backyard. There is no world beyond the fences; the persimmon tree marks the border and beyond it everything is strange and unfamiliar. All that I know, all that I need is here. In time, the perpetual questioning will end and my mind will grow quiet. Maybe then I will let this place fall over me, soft and warm like a blanket.

My mother calls to me to come back in and help with breakfast. She is opening a carton of eggs on the counter and counts out a half dozen. "Would you put some butter in the pan on the front burner?" she asks me. "And put some more bread in the toaster for yourself. There's an English muffin, if you'd like."

We will eat the years. "Toast is fine," I say. I finger the lever of the sparkling four-slice Sunbeam. "New toaster?" I ask.

"Birthday present from your father," she says, cracking the eggs into a bowl. "Last month."

"Last month?" I ask her.

She is beating the eggs vigorously, the bowl braced against her hip. "March fourth," she says. "Works real good. Can't understand how we put up with that old one for all those years. Toast burnt one morning, pale the next." She hands me a knife and pushes a stick of butter in my direction.

A thick slice of butter melts and bubbles in the pan. My mother pours in the eggs. They sizzle. She uses the fork to pull the cooking eggs away from the sides of the pan. They grow firm. I am struck by the mystery of this simple act, cooking scrambled eggs. "Do you still like them dry?" she asks. I try to remember the scrambled eggs I have eaten over the last ten years, and whether or not I noticed if I liked them one way or the other. "If you don't answer me soon, you're not going to have a choice," my mother says. She turns her head to face me.

"Yes. Please."

Jessie comes back into the kitchen and takes her place at the table, looking a little timid. My mother gives the eggs one more turn. The toast is ready. I spread a napkin across my lap while my mother serves the eggs. She pours the water for the tea, sets the milk on the table, and takes her seat. After a private grace she passes a small bowl of preserves to me. "You still like strawberry jam?" she asks.

"Yes, ma'am," I say.

"And your tea with milk?"

Tea with milk sounds so polite, so genteel. Cups and saucers, the same china every day, every meal. Jessie lifts her fork filled with eggs halfway to her mouth. Then she looks at her grandmother for a sign that it's all right to begin. My mother gives her a little nod. Still, Jessie waits to see what her grandmother will do, taking a bite of toast and a sip of tea like a vigilant and soon-to-be genteel echo of my mother. "Milk?" I ask my mother, as though I'd forgotten what it was.

"Do you want a little milk in your tea?" she asks patiently.

"No, I don't think so. I mean," I stutter, "I'm not really sure."

"No hurry," she says.

It takes all I have to swallow one mouthful of scrambled eggs. I cannot chew at all, and then the wet lump has to find its own way down my throat. Jessie and my mother are talking about the park a couple of blocks away, my park, Teddy's and mine, about our swimming pool and the arts-and-crafts hut. For a moment, their faces look flat and their voices sound hollow and far away. Then they both turn rosy, golden and pink.

Acknowledgments

I've heard that there are people who write alone, who neither seek nor receive the ready ear or willing spirit of friends to make the story come to life outside their circus-minds. I could never do that. And because of these people, I didn't have to: my patient early readers, Jackie Rothenberg and Deborah Proos, who were amazed, as I was, that I could invent a story; the steady avid readers, Julie Erickson, Elaine Parker, Meredith Tredeau, and Susan Streitfeld, who watched over the writing of these stories like angels guarding the dreams of my night; the painters who both read my work and shared with me the trembling ground of their processes, Robert Farber, Francis Hines, Dennis O'Sullivan, and Bob Carvin, who, with Bill Oster, made their homes a place where my work began to live in the world; the other writers—Graciela Vidal, Jim Gould, and the women of City College—whose work gave life to my own; the PEN American Center and the judges of the 1989 Nelson Algren Competition, for the encouragement without which others manage but this writer might not have; Stephen Pascal, who gave me heart when I had no heart for writing; and Toinette Lippe, my friend, F. Joseph Spieler, my agent, and David Rosenthal, my editor, who ushered me into the world of books like a welcome guest for whom a place at the table had long been set.

ABOUT THE AUTHOR

SUSAN THAMES was born in Roanoke, Virginia,
and now lives and teaches in Brooklyn, New York.